Frederic knows he is too old for Sarah...

"That's not a good idea, Sarah," he said huskily. He felt her trembling body close to his, and once again suppressed a deep desire to take her in his arms. "You...you'd better go home now."

"Am I interfering with your work?" Sarah asked in a disappointed tone. "I only wanted to help."

"I know you did and I appreciate it. But I can't do my work when I get distracted. Run along now."

Sarah climbed on Star and headed home. *"Run along," he said. Like I was a child pestering him. That's all I am to him—a child. That's all I'll ever be, no matter how old I get.* She did not look back at him once. *I've learned my lesson. I won't pester him again.*

Frederic watched her ride away, then turned back to his task with a heavy heart. "What's a fella to do?" he sighed. "I can't fight these feelings much longer. Sarah Jane is so lovely. Whenever she's near me, all I can think about is pulling her into my arms. If only she weren't so young. . ."

CAROL MASON PARKER lives in northern Michigan. She is a wife and mother of four grown children. *Haven of Peace* is her first inspirational romance.

Haven
of Peace

Carol Mason Parker

Heartsong Presents

A note from the Author:

To my husband, Herb, for all his love, patience, and encouragement.

With special thanks to our daughter, Kimberly Parker Christmas, for transferring my completed manuscript onto computer disks.

I love to hear from my readers! You may write to me at the following address:

Carol Mason Parker
Author Relations
P.O. Box 719
Uhrichsville, OH 44683

ISBN 1-55748-591-7

HAVEN OF PEACE

PRINTED IN THE U.S.A.

forward

Although this is a novel of fiction, some of the characters are real people and some of the facts are true. This story was written in memory of my great-grandfather, Captain Frederic T. Mason, (1844-1909). Captain Fred served with the Union Army in the Civil War, and this book is dedicated to all his descendents.

Carol Mason Parker

Waterville

Within Her gates doth Wisdom sit enthroned,
The sceptre governs with its gentle sway;
And Plenty smiles through all Her woodland aisles,
Blest is the coming of the perfect day.
We may not pledge thee in the sparkling wine,
Since Bacchus doth no place of honor fill;
But here's a health in nectar old as Time,
Whose name is linked with thine. . .sweet Water(ville)

—*anonymous*

(Taken from the *Old Waterville* picture book, and used by permission of the Waterville Historical Society, Waterville, Maine.)

one

A peaceful hush flooded the countryside. It was early July, 1865, and three short months since the bitter war between the North and South. Frederic Mason shifted the haversack on his shoulder as he limped along the dusty, gravel road leading to his family's farm in Waterville, Maine.

His right leg, the one with the ball still in the thigh, started to drag, and he needed to rest. A huge elm tree by the side of the road beckoned and provided welcome shade as he lowered his weary body into the tall grass. Leaning against the elm's rough bark, he rubbed his hand up and down, massaging the wounded leg. He untied the bandanna from his neck and wiped huge beads of sweat from his face and brow.

He had been wounded April 9th, the last day of the war. His company, the 11th Maine, under General Edward Ord, had pushed toward the Confederate line and seen the roofs of the hamlet of Appomattox Court House in the distance. The gallant Lieutenant Colonel Jonathon A. Hill, his regiment's immediate commander, was told to close and hold the pike.

"Charge that battery!" Colonel Hill had shouted, pointing to the Confederate forces on the ridge across the field. Frederic's regiment had sprung from the woods into an open field, meeting a barrage of grape shot and bullets.

Remembering brought tears to Frederic's eyes. His close friend, hit with a bullet in the chest, had screamed and fallen to the ground. Frederic had knelt beside him, cradling his head in his arms. Helplessly, he had watched his friend die.

"Goodbye, ole buddy", he whispered, then jumped to his feet, his stomach tied in knots and his eyes brimming with tears.

Midway across the field, grape shot and shrapnel had hit his right thigh, knocking him unconscious. He learned later that Lieutenant Colonel Hill had been injured in the same battle.

Frederic remembered being transferred to a hospital in Chesapeake, Virginia, his thigh full of shrapnel which had shattered the bone and caused the right leg to shorten. One ball they were unable to remove. It would remain with him, a constant reminder of a nation torn apart, each side dedicated to its own cause.

The war was finally over, though, and he was back home again. Now, he could pick up his life. Get back on the farm and work with his pa and grandpa. Marry Becky Sue, just like he'd promised all those years ago before he'd left for the war. Thinking of Becky Sue, he smiled; soon, very soon, he would see her again. He hadn't heard from her, not since he was wounded, he remembered, and his smile flickered, but no doubt her letters had been held up.

As if in answer to his thoughts, a lone rider approached on horseback, startling Frederic out of his daydreams.

"Hullo there!" A large-framed, middle-aged man peered down at Frederic from his horse. "Well, if it ain't young Fred Mason jest back from the war! Almost didn't recognize ya with the mustache ya growed. Does yer Pappy know yer comin'?"

Frederic stood to his feet and smiled. "Nice to see you, Mr. Collins." He took a deep breath and extended his hand to Becky Sue's father. "No, the folks don't know I'm coming. I wanted to surprise everyone. The hospital released me quicker than expected. I just got into town on the noon train and felt like walking home."

"Yep," Hiram Collins eyed Frederic's bad leg, "peers ya were able ta keep the leg after all. Back in April talk was that ya'd lose it shore enough."

"The Lord's been good, Mr. Collins. The leg's still with me. . .just dragging a little."

"Reckon yer pap will be mighty glad ta have ya home in time fer harvest." Hiram Collins squinted a little in the bright sun as he peered down his long nose at Frederic. "Bet yer shore glad to get out of the army."

Frederic pulled his twenty-one-year-old body up to its full six feet. His dark hair, damp with perspiration, curled around his face like a child's, but his blue eyes were a man's. "My papers state, 'Captain Fred Mason honorably discharged on account of wounds at Appomattox Court House,' sir. But I'm thankful the war is over and our great nation is one again. Being away for three years made me mighty anxious to get home." He hesitated a moment. "Sir, how's Becky Sue? She never wrote me in the hospital."

"Yep, yer letters came ta the house." Hiram Collins frowned as he spoke. "Becky Sue run off and married Zack Turner right after she heered about yer leg. Broke her ma's heart too. She was plannin' on a nice church weddin', her bein' our oldest daughter and all."

Frederic's face turned ashen and tears brimmed his eyes. Clumsily, he wiped a hand across his face. When he finally spoke, his voice was halted and broken. "But, sir, we were promised. Becky Sue promised to wait for me until after the war."

"I know, boy," Hiram Collins admitted, "and I'm right sorry about it. Thought yer folks had writ ya, but maybe they thought totherwise, ya bein' in the hospital and all."

Frederic's frame slumped as he sat down on the edge of the road, his head in his hands. Sobs racked his body as he fought for control.

"Anythin' I can do fer ya?" Mr. Collins asked kindly as he got down from his horse. "Let me take yer sack there and other belongin's to yer place."

"I'll be okay, sir," Fred said hoarsely as he waved him aside. "Thanks for offering your help. Guess I'll just get along now. It's not much farther and I'm sure anxious to get home."

Hiram Collins mounted his mare, touched his hand to his hat, and rode off. He knew Frederic needed to be alone with his thoughts.

The Collins' property butted up to the Mason spread on one side. Often the men had helped one another during harvest season, while the women sewed, canned, and quilted. Fred and his sisters, Cassie and Emily, had walked to the little red schoolhouse with the Collins children, Becky Sue, Billy Bob, and later on little golden-haired Sarah Jane.

Becky Sue's face flashed before him, and in his mind he saw her dark flowing hair and sparkling green eyes. They had both been eighteen when he had joined up, proud to serve his country. "The Union must be preserved at any cost," he'd told her. "But I'll be back, Becky Sue. Mr. Lincoln will have this war over in no time." Frederic had drawn her close and whispered against her silky dark hair. "I love you. I've always loved you, even when we were kids. Will you be my wife, Becky Sue? Will you marry me when I get back?"

Frederic could almost hear her soft voice and feel her clinging arms. "Oh yes, yes, yes, Frederic! We'll be married as soon as you get home. I'll be waiting for you, if it takes forever!"

"How long is forever?" Frederic mumbled to himself now.

Her "forever" hadn't even lasted three years. He felt tired and empty inside, but he ignored his bad leg and quickened his step a little. He wanted to be home now, wanted to be with his own people and see the love in their eyes. They could not take away the wound that Becky Sue had dealt him, he knew, but they were the only thing left to him now.

Still, the pain in his heart eased just a little as he looked across the green hills toward his family's land. How he loved this countryside with its woods and graceful trees. Tall spruce and pine, along with birch, maple, oak, and elm, lined the narrow country road. A wave of feeling washed over him. "This is my kind of country," he mused. "This is where I belong."

Just around the next bend, Frederic saw the large, white farmhouse his grandpa had built for his bride on the rolling hundred acres. The house sat back from the road a good piece, on a hill overlooking the surrounding area. Farming had always been a way of life for the Mason family, and now Frederic saw the cattle and horses grazing on the hillside with the tall outbuildings just beyond.

Frederic knew every inch of this land. He knew it by heart and loved every part of it. Many times he had visualized these scenes during the past three years, wondering if he would ever see home and family again. "Terrible waste, this war!" he muttered. "Many didn't make it. Young men blown apart, others like myself crippled for life. Boys turned into men overnight. Some of us became hard and bitter, others callous and indifferent."

Frederic remembered those who had found the horrors of war so dreadful they were unable to cope. When the going had gotten too tough, they'd deserted their posts and filtered away into the woods, weakening the ranks. Frederic shook his head. "Yep, war brings out the best and worst in men. Much as I hated the killing, I'm thankful it didn't make me bitter. It's only by God's grace I'm alive today."

He squinted in the sun as he looked toward the homestead. "The war is over and I'm home at last. But, God," his whisper was filled with pain, "What do I have to live for now? Becky Sue is married to someone else. Help me, God. Help me be able to bear it."

two

With a deep breath, Frederic shifted his haversack and started up the long, gravel drive to his family home. Large trees dotted the front yard that sloped toward the house. "I reckon it looks just the same," Fred murmured as he paused a moment to let his eyes drink in the scene.

The clapboard house, with its green shutters and huge chimneys, was etched clearly against the azure sky. Small-paned windows, gingerbread trim, and steep gables and dormers made the house look as though it were trimmed with diamonds and points of lace. A summer porch ran across the front of the house and wrapped itself around the side. Everything was just as he remembered; even the wooden swing his grandpa had made was still in place.

Laddie, the collie, began barking furiously as Fred continued up the long drive. Suddenly, Laddie stopped barking and met Fred halfway, his tail wagging. The dog jumped in delight at having his old friend home.

Fred knelt down and gathered the dog to him. "Lad, old boy. It's good to see you," he murmured into the dog's soft furry coat. He patted the noble head and stroked the soft ears. Laddie rolled over so he could rub his belly. "You're getting fat, old fellow." The dog danced and ran in circles as the two of them headed for the house.

"Fred, is thet you?" Grandpa Caleb sat on the porch in his old wicker rocker, sipping a glass of cool apple cider. He pulled himself slowly up to greet his only grandson, and Fred noticed how much older and grayer he seemed. He knew his grandma had died of pneumonia two years back while he was away at the war.

"Gramps!" he cried as he flung his arms around the old man. "Gramps, how I've missed you. I'm so sorry about Grandma."

After a quiet moment, Caleb spoke. "The Lord wanted her real bad, Fred. She's with Him now. There's an empty place here, thet's fer sure." The elder Mason touched his heart. Then his face brightened. "But we'll see her agin, one day."

Fred's eyes filled with tears, not only for his dear little Grandma Mason, but also for Becky Sue who was lost to him forever.

"Yer ma's inside, Fred. She'll be fit ta be tied. Yer pa's out on the back property fixin' fences. Always so much ta do and I'm no help taday with this confounded lumbago actin' up. My joints ache and pain most of the time. But listen ta me, would ya? Yer the one thet's hurtin'. How's that leg doin'? Ya shouldn't a walked from town, boy. We coulda brung the wagon fer ya."

"No, I wanted to see everything slowly, Gramps, and drink it all in. I was so thirsty for this land, every tree, every trail, the rolling hills. There were times I thought I'd never see any of this again."

"Land-a-goshen, Frederic!" Mary Jane Mason came bustling out the kitchen door onto the porch. A small, stout woman with hazel eyes, she pulled her brown hair straight back into a bun at the nape of her neck. Her round face beamed and her pink cheeks flushed with excitement. "My boy! My boy! Yer home safe!"

Fred had to stoop as she gathered him to her bosom, her whole body convulsed with sobs. "But, oh Frederic, yer poor leg. We've worried so about ya."

"Ma, don't cry. My leg's fine. I'm alright, honest. I'm tired from my trip but I'm home now. That's what counts."

Mrs. Mason released him and wiped her eyes on her checkered apron. "Let me look at ya, son. Ya sure are a sight fer these eyes. We're all so proud of ya. We prayed every day, and thank the Lord yer safe. Now ya jest rest some in the swing while I get ya somethin' ta eat."

"Thanks, Ma," Fred said as he slumped his body onto the swing.

Mrs. Mason reappeared shortly with a pitcher of apple cider and a plate of sandwiches. "This will hold ya till supper. Yer pa will be back from the fields about six. Some of the cattle were gettin' out of the pasture and he found the spot. Grandpa helped him yesterday. Taday he's jest finishin' up."

"Where's Cassie and Emily? Are they away?"

"It's a wonder ya didn't pass 'em on the road," Grandpa said. "They went ta town in the buggy hours ago."

"They needed ribbon and dress material," Ma offered, "and I needed some staples. They like an excuse ta go fer me, but they should be back soon."

"I guess they are young ladies by now," Fred exclaimed between mouthfuls. "When I left, they were just my 'little sisters.'"

"Yep, not so little anymore," Grandpa agreed. "Leastwise they think they're growed up, bein' seventeen and eighteen. Can't keep 'em young forever."

"And I suppose they've been courted by some of the local fellas too?" Fred asked.

Before his grandfather could answer, the family buggy, pulled by old Nell, flew up the drive. Two girls dressed in calico, giggling and laden with packages, stepped out. Fred left the swing and hurried, limping, to meet them.

"It's Fred!" they screamed simultaneously. Packages flew

everywhere as they hugged Fred and fired questions at the same time.

"Cassie! Emily! You sure grew up on me." Fred held them admiringly at arm's length. "How come you grew up so fast?"

"You've been away a long time, big brother," Cassie said teasingly.

"We just growed!" Emily laughed. "It was easy!"

Grandpa Caleb cared for old Nell while the girls chattered constantly, filling Frederic in on all the local news. He listened to some sad information about friends killed in the war, and his heart ached as mentally he relived the horrors of his own experiences at Petersburg and Appomattox.

"There's been lots of weddings since the war ended," Emily was saying. Suddenly she faltered as Cassie shook her head and gave her a meaningful look. Fred's face became drawn and tight.

"It's alright, little sisters," he said gravely. "I already heard about Becky Sue. Mr. Collins met me on the road, down a piece. I could see that it bothered him to tell me."

"It's terrible of her!" Emily exploded. "Downright mean! She's just so fickle and two-faced, I declare!"

"Now, Emily, be kind," Mrs. Mason warned. "It's done and over and we can't change it a whit. This kinda talk won't help Fred none. Son, we wanted ta spare ya the news as long as we could." Seeing his downcast expression, she added, "I'm sure ya want ta wash up and rest a bit before supper. We can all talk some more then."

"I would, Ma, thanks," Frederic replied, and headed inside. The pain in his injured leg was surpassed only by the throb in his heart. His entire body screamed out in pain over the loss of Becky Sue to another.

"Why, God? First my leg and now this. Becky Sue couldn't stand the idea of being married to a cripple!" He spat out the words and they choked in his throat. "Ma knows how hard it hurts," he sighed as he settled himself back in his old room.

The room was just as he'd left it, the same single bed with the patch quilt his grandma made him when he was a boy. Lovingly, he fingered the quilt, so full of memories. Across the room stood a pine dresser and commode, with bowl, pitcher, and kerosene lamp. Grandpa had crafted the furniture from huge pine trees on the family property. Most of the furniture in the house had been made by his pa and grandpa. They were craftsmen, both of them.

Fred had the same inner desire to work with wood. He remembered his grandpa helping him make a pine cutting board, shaped like a pig, when he was ten years old. It was to be a gift for his mother's birthday, but he made a wrong cut, messed up the shape of the pig, and it was lopsided. Then he refused to give it to her.

"It's ruined, Grandpa, it's ruined!" Fred moaned as he hid the board behind some scraps of lumber.

"Now, Freddy, yer ma'll love it jest the same because ya made it, boy," Grandpa insisted. "Don't ya go a hidin' it on her."

Later his mother found it, loved it, and didn't care a whit that it was crooked. She only cared that it was from her boy.

Frederic took off his dusty clothes, washed up, and threw back the quilt. As he stretched out on the neat pine bed he whispered, "Ma knew how bad I felt then and she knows now. Ma always knows when I'm hurting."

three

"Son, wake up!" Frederic's father shook him gently. "Fred boy. . .ya've come home ta us."

Fred opened his eyes to see his pa's face smiling down at him. Chase Mason was an older copy of Fred: the same dark hair, though now touched with gray, the same deep blue eyes that squinted when he smiled, the same tall, lean frame that knew hard work from farming. "Pa!" Fred's voice broke as the elder Mason embraced his son.

"Come on boy, Ma's got supper on the table. Let's get it while it's hot."

Supper was a joyous occasion. Ma prepared two of their choice hens, along with dumplings, Boston baked beans, johnny cake, and apple pie. "Fit fer a king!" Grandpa exclaimed patting his belly.

"Ma," Fred said, "I dreamed of your cooking for three long years while away at the war. I have to say it, your cooking just gets better and better."

"Pshaw, Fred," Mary Jane Mason said. "It's jest plain cookin'. It does do my heart good ta see ya eat so well, son."

After the meal, Chase took the worn family Bible and read a portion of Scripture. Their family custom included meditating on God's Word each evening and having a time of prayer. Grandpa Caleb prayed this time, waxing eloquent in thanking God for His bountiful blessings. "And thank ya, Lord, fer bringin' our Fred boy home ta us. In Jesus name, amen."

Now the family besieged Fred with questions. They were eager to hear about his experiences in the war. He talked for

18

some time, but kept the horrors of war brief and omitted much of the pain and sorrow.

"But yer leg, son. Is it terribly painful to ya?" his mother asked.

"I'm just thankful I could keep it, Ma. At first the doc said I'd lose it for sure. There's no pain now, unless I get over-tired, but even that will go away the doctor said. It's just a nuisance to me, that's all."

While Mrs. Mason and the girls cleared the table, the men continued their discussion in the parlor.

"Pa, what a tragedy about Mr. Lincoln being shot. It made me angry when I heard about the killing while in the hospital. It makes no sense. . .no sense at all."

"Abe Lincoln was a good man," Chase agreed. "A warm and understandin' president, even brilliant the way he held this nation tagether. But there are still strong and bitter feelings against him, especially in the South."

"It's right hard to understand why he was killed," Grandpa interjected. "But God, in His plan, knows all about it. He's the One that's in control."

"Some people say we're in a depression. Is that right, Pa?"

"Well, son, we never had prosperity," Chase answered. "So how can we have a depression?"

While Mrs. Mason put away the food, Cassie and Emily quickly did up the dishes. "When can I tell Fred about Bill and me?" Cassie asked her ma. "Bill's coming around to-night, courting."

"It will hurt him, Cassie," her mother warned.

"Ma, the wedding's in September, so I have to tell him." Cassie's hazel eyes clouded as she shook her chestnut curls. She had tied yellow ribbons in her hair to match her dress of calico and muslin.

"Fred must be told," Mrs. Mason sighed. "I jest hope it

don't hurt him too badly. He's been hurt so much already."

"Bill's coming!" Emily shouted as Laddie started barking and a lone rider appeared galloping up the long drive.

Cassie patted her hair, pinched her cheeks, and fairly flew off the porch to meet him. How grand and tall he looked, she thought as he swung his lean body down and tied his gray gelding to the hitching post. Bill Collins had a thatch of reddish-gold hair, bright blue eyes, and a smile that lit up his whole face. Cassie greeted him warmly, and they walked together hand in hand toward the porch swing.

"You're pretty as can be in that yellow dress, Cassie. I'm sure glad you're my girl."

Cassie's cheeks burned under his steady gaze. "You are a flatterer, Bill."

"It's true, Cassie. . .it's the honest truth."

"Oh, Bill." She went into his arms and lifted her face to his.

After a moment, she drew away and led him onto the porch. "Frederic's inside," she said. "You'll have to talk to him before you leave. It's so good to have him home safe at last."

"How is he?"

"He seems okay. He limps. And he's quieter than before. But he's still the same Frederic."

"Pa said he took the news about Becky Sue hard."

Cassie nodded. "He hasn't said much. But you can see he's hurting bad."

Bill shook his head. "I know she's my own sister, but I can't understand what got into her. I know she was scared when she heard Fred was going to lose his leg. But why did she have to up and marry Zack so fast? You'd think she didn't have a brain in her head. What a thing to do to a guy just back from fighting for our country. Fred deserved better, and that's the truth."

"I know, Bill, I know."

They sat close together in the porch swing, silent, thinking of Frederic. After a few moments, though, they turned toward each other once again, and soon they had entered their own small world. They talked softly, oblivious to anyone in the house.

"Pa and I have the cabin almost done, Cassie," Bill said. "You haven't seen it since it was roughed in. I wish you'd come see it tomorrow. You need to tell us how you want some of the finishing done. That's your department. Let Emily come with you if she wants to."

"I will, Bill," Cassie replied eagerly. "I've been meaning to come for quite a spell, but just been so busy with my sewing. My wedding dress is done. I have two more dresses to make and then I'll start on curtains. It's such fun planning our own place." Cassie squeezed his hand and laid her head on his shoulder. "Look at that moon coming up, Bill, just for us."

The couple sat in silence for several minutes, their hearts full of love and bursting with plans for their future. The swing creaked and groaned as they rocked back and forth, back and forth. Laddie was curled up in one corner of the porch fast asleep, while fireflies darted here and there, dancing in the twilight.

The men finished their lengthy discussion in the parlor. Grandpa yawned and excused himself. "This old man needs his sleep," he muttered and headed upstairs. Chase and Fred stepped out on the porch for a breath of fresh air.

"Mr. Mason, sir." Bill jumped to his feet. "Fred! Heard you were back. Good to see you." He held out his hand.

"Billy Bob!" Fred squinted in the twilight. "Say, are you courting my sister, Cassie?"

"Yep, I been courting her nigh on a year now. We're both

eighteen and your pa gave his permission. We plan to be married come September."

"Pa, is that true? Cassie. . .you never told me. My letters said nothing about it."

Cassie slid off the swing and put her arms around her brother. "I. . .I wouldn't let them tell, Fred. It was to be a surprise. Bill and I wanted to have a double wedding with you and Becky Sue." Her last words faded as she moved away. "I'm sorry, Fred, so sorry."

"Don't worry about that none, Cassie," Frederic mumbled quickly. "I'm happy for you and Bill." He shook Bill's hand and slapped him on the back. "Congratulations, Billy Bob. You have yourself a special girl there. Take care of her."

"You bet I will," Bill Collins said heartily as he drew Cassie close.

"It's gettin' late, Cassie," Mr. Mason warned. "We best be gettin' inside."

"I'll be leaving, sir. Good night." Bill Collins moved toward the steps.

"Pa, I'll be coming in just a few minutes," Cassie said.

A full moon cast its lengthening shadows on the young couple as they walked hand in hand toward Bill's gelding. Trees silhouetted against the soft sky seemed to whisper their good nights.

"I feel badly for Frederic," Cassie stated. "We're so happy, and he's hurting so."

Bill cupped her small oval face in his large, rough hands and looked into her hazel eyes. The moonlight lit her face with a silver glow.

"I know, Cassie, and I feel bad too. But we can't change what's happened. Life goes on and we make the best of it. Frederic is strong. He'll make out fine. We just have to trust God."

four

Fred awoke early the next morning before any in the household were up. The light from the full moon penetrated his room and he dressed quickly. Silently, he crept from the house, nudged Laddie where he slept on the porch, and headed for the back pasture. Laddie trotted beside him, delighted at this early morning walk. Down the trail they went, the young man and his dog, with the towering trees rising around them in the fading darkness. The trail led around a bend, then through the smooth clay fields before coming to the creek.

"This is my favorite spot, quiet and secluded," he said aloud. "I like the peacefulness of the countryside where I can mull things over."

He lowered himself to the ground with his back against a giant maple. The ground had a fresh, sweet smell and was moist and spongy from a heavy dew. The solitude was broken only by bird song and the low sounds of the cattle grazing in the field.

"Kinda wet, eh, Laddie?" He nuzzled the dog's head and scratched his ears. Laddie laid his head on Fred's lap as if to say "all's right with the world." The creek bubbled and gurgled on its way downstream. It was shallow and narrow at this point but broadened out and got deeper further back.

"This is nice," Frederic said. "Far away from the bloody battlefields and smell of the dying. I wish I could get it out of my mind."

Presently the sun started to rise on the horizon. "Look at that ball of fire, Laddie. What a sight for these eyes. There's nothing prettier, nowhere!"

A twig snapped and Laddie jumped to his feet.

"So here you are, Fred! I knew I'd find you here." Emily sat down by her brother in the damp grass, pulling her skirts around her. "This has always been our special place."

"Look at that sunrise, Emily! God splashes His flaming color against the bluest of skies. It's to remind us of Himself and His goodness to all His creatures."

"What goodness?" Emily snapped, her blue eyes flashing. "Is it good that you have a crippled leg? Is it good about Becky Sue breaking her promise, running off and marrying someone else? I declare. . .God doesn't seem very good sometimes at all. Why does He let these terrible things happen?"

"I can't answer that, Emily. God is God. He is perfect. I love Becky Sue and I'm fighting bitter feelings. I've asked God why it happened. He let me keep my leg and my life. I'm not bitter about the war, but I feel bitter toward Becky Sue. She betrayed my trust."

Suddenly Emily, tomboy that she was, took off her shoes and stockings, gathered her cotton skirts to her knees, and started across the creek, jumping from one rock to another. "Come on, Fred," she called. "Get a move on!"

Fred quickly took off his shoes and stockings, rolled up his pant legs, and followed her cautiously, favoring his injured leg. He lost his balance more easily now, but he made it safely to the other side. Laddie splashed his way through the creek and proceeded to shake himself, spraying Fred and Emily with the cold, clear water.

"Hey, Laddie!" Fred and Emily sat down on the mossy bank amidst the clover and wild daisies, laughing.

"I'm glad you are home, Fred. Will you stay and help Pa and Gramps with the farm? It's getting harder all the time for Grandpa to keep up." Emily's blue eyes searched his.

"Yep," he drawled. "Farming's inborn in me. I've been waiting three years to get back to this." Fred gestured toward the surrounding landscape. "There's something about working with the soil, just feeling it in your hands, planting crops and seeing them grow. And the animals. . .well, they're like friends. What about you, little sister? Do you have a beau, too, like Cassie? Will you be getting married on me one day?"

"Nobody around here catches my fancy!" Emily declared emphatically. "I don't want to be a farmer's wife like Ma, and like Cassie will be. I'm tired of farm life. . .I want to live in town. I want to do something with my life. I'll marry a rich fella maybe, if I ever decide to marry. Ma says I can take a teachers' course at Colby College while staying with Aunt Maudie in town. Aunt Maude's so lonely now that Uncle George passed on, and no kids of their own."

"Can Aunt Maude put up with that hot temper of yours?" Fred teased.

Emily pushed Fred affectionately. "It's better now than it was. I'm more grown up."

"Well, I remember those times when you were so mad you'd hold your breath until you fainted."

"Yep, and I remember what you and Cassie did to me."

Fred laughed. "You were about nine I guess the last time you held your breath like that. You were madder than ever just because you couldn't have your own way. Cassie and I picked you up and dumped you head first in the rain barrel."

"Ma was real mad at you, too. She said I might have drowned."

"Naw. We just dunked you up and down a few times, fast like. We didn't hold you down. It cured you, too, didn't it? You never held your breath after that."

"I got over it. . .but who wouldn't after such horrid treatment?"

Fred was thoughtful a few minutes. "Billy Bob seems like a fine young man. He grew up while I was away. I guess he and Cassie will be mighty happy."

"Bill is nice," Emily agreed. "He and his pa are building a cabin for Bill and Cassie on a piece of the Collins' property. Cassie is so excited. She wants me to ride over with her this afternoon to see it. It's going to be different with Cassie gone. That's another reason I want to go away. I'll miss her."

"She'll only be a short ways off. You could see her any time. It won't change that much."

"Yep, it will. . .it will change. It will be mighty different with her being married. She won't be my playmate anymore. We've always been so close, being just eleven months apart. Like twins sorta, Ma always said. Now she'll have Bill. He doesn't like being called Billy Bob anymore. Anyway, I'd just be in the way."

Their thoughts were broken by the tolling of the old dinner bell. Ma used it whenever they were to come, for a meal or whatever. This time it meant breakfast so they hurried across the creek, put on their shoes and stockings, and started up the trail. An aroma of fried bacon reached their nostrils as they rounded the last bend.

Fred sniffed deeply. The sweet morning air, punctuated with the smell of coffee and crisp bacon, saturated his being. "If God's heaven was on earth, Emily, this would sure be it!"

five

Breakfast was a sturdy meal at the Mason farm. Oatmeal with fresh cream, molasses doughnuts, and Ma's homemade blackberry preserves started it off. Then bacon and eggs followed with huge mugs of strong coffee. Fully satisfied, the men left for chores while the women folk set to theirs.

Fred eagerly fed the pigs and chickens, watered them from the spring, and checked on the horses and cattle in the pasture. Then he worked the garden, down the rows of beans and into the corn. He loved the smell of the earth as he turned it over again and again. The carrots and onions were half grown and little green tomatoes hung from the vines in abundance. "It will be a good harvest," he muttered.

After the noon meal, the elder male Masons took Fred out to their work place in an old log shed. On one side sat the huge bellows and tools used to shoe the horses. The other half of the shed contained lumber and wood-working tools. They had been working on a four poster bed for Cassie and Bill's wedding gift.

"It's beautiful!" Fred exclaimed, running his hand over the smooth pine posts. "Has Cassie seen it?"

"Not yet. We've warned her ta stay away till it's done. Jest a little more sandin' and then the finishin' stain. Grandpa does all the finish work," Chase explained. "He's the real craftsman."

"You've made this shed into a dandy workshop," Fred stated as he glanced around. There were wooden swings, tables, chests, and baby cradles partly assembled. "What do you do

27

with all these?"

"We sell them ta neighbors and town folk who hear about our work. In late September we'll take 'em into Waterville ta the fair. Ma sells her preserves and pickles, and Grandpa and I sell our wood pieces. The ladies also sell a few patch quilts and some fancy work. Gives us some extra money fer the long winter."

"I want to do this," Fred said seriously. "Do you think I could learn this trade?" He caressed the fine pieces and inhaled deeply, letting the odor of the new wood linger in his nostrils. "Working with wood is the next best thing to working with the soil."

"Sure ya could, Fred, and ya'd be good at it too. Maybe ya could make us some bread boards fer the fair, shaped like pigs," Grandpa suggested with a sly smile.

Fred and his pa laughed heartily.

"I'll do it," Fred agreed. "Pigs are my favorite for bread boards, if I can just make them so they aren't lopsided."

"It's good ta see ya laugh, son," Chase said. "Grandpa and me hoped ya'd have a hankerin' ta work with wood. We got kinda a trade goin' here that ya might like ta carry on. There's enough timber still ta be cut on the property, more than we need fer the wood stove and fireplaces. We figger there's ample ta spare fer woodworkin'."

"Can't think of anything I'd rather do. I'm anxious to start."

"Are ya sure ya want ta work the farm, Fred, and jest stay here?" Chase asked seriously. "Yer ma wondered if ya might want to go to Colby and get some more book learnin'. Emily's got that idea in her head, says she wants ta get away and get some schoolin'."

"I'll leave that for Emily, Pa. My heart is here on the farm, working the soil, tending the cattle, and learning the woodcrafting. This is the only place I want to be."

"We sure do need ya, boy." Grandpa placed gnarled hands on his grandson's shoulders. "Ya don't know how bad yer needed, or how long we've wished it."

"It's settled then," Fred said. "You need me, and I need you. We'll work side by side on this great land that God has given us. We'll plant and He'll give us the increase, teaching us a few lessons besides."

The two elder Masons showed relief at Fred's decision. Being native "down-easters," they were a tough and independent lot. They would never have pressed Frederic to stay on the farm, but they were glad that for Frederic, like for themselves, the greatest joy came from wrestling with the land.

In the early afternoon Cassie and Emily took the buggy and old Nell over the land that led to the back of the Collins' property where Bill and his father were building the cabin. Timber had been cleared and the cabin sat on a little knoll with a view of the countryside. Bill and Mr. Collins heard them coming and hurried out to greet them.

"It's beautiful, Bill!" Cassie exclaimed. "Oh, Mr. Collins, thank you. I love it, I really do."

"I'm glad you like it, Cassie," Bill said as he placed an arm around her tiny waist. "It's ready now for the woman's touch."

He walked her through the rooms: a large kitchen, living room, and two bedrooms. "We can add on as our family grows," he said shyly. "We'll have a bigger place later on." They were lost in their own little world.

"How do ya like it, Emily?" Mr. Collins asked as she lingered behind.

"It's nice, Mr. Collins. You and Bill have worked very hard, I can tell. It's the perfect house for Cassie."

"But do you like it?" he persisted.

"I like it for her, but not for me. I want to be in town. I want to be with people," Emily said honestly.

"So that's it," Mr. Collins smiled. "The country girl wants ta leave the country, spread her wings a little, is that it?"

"I plan to attend Colby, the liberal arts college in Waterville, and live with my Aunt Maude. That will suit me a whole lot better than staying here."

Cassie, captivated by the smooth logs of the cabin's walls, didn't let her sister's remarks dampen her spirits. She looked out the front window at a view of wild apple trees, clumps of birches, and fields of blowing daisies. Deftly, she set about measuring the windows for curtains.

"I'll make them quicker than you can shake a stick," she exclaimed. "I have yellow calico for the kitchen and blue for the living room. And one bedroom will have blue and the other yellow. They're my favorite colors."

Cassie and Bill planned where they would put their furniture. They had very little, but each set of parents gave them extra pieces from their attics. The poster bed was to be a wedding gift, and they could count on a cradle later on when needed. The womenfolk made scores of dish towels, rag rugs, and bed quilts.

Bill and Cassie walked out onto the porch. "This house doesn't need a thing," Cassie insisted as she turned to Bill and their eyes met.

"I can think of something important," Bill said softly.

"What does it need?" Cassie smiled saucily up at him.

"Only you, my darling," he whispered in her ear. "It won't be complete until you are here."

six

The weary days of harvest were at hand. As quickly as the men harvested the crops, the womenfolk canned them. Nothing could compare with their sweet corn. The thick blanket of snow in winter was part of the reason for the sweetness of Maine's corn crop. Wild berries that grew in abundance on the hillside were carefully picked and made into jellies and preserves. They stacked the field corn in corn cribs and pitched hay into huge mounds by the barn. They would have enough to feed the animals through the long, hard winter ahead.

Everyone was involved. The hard work helped Frederic heal, saturating his being like a tonic. He liked being busy and drove himself constantly. He wanted no time to think about Becky Sue.

He had seen her at a distance at church a few times, but he avoided meeting her face to face. When she headed toward him, he bolted for the door. Seeing her in the flesh and knowing she belonged to another was just too painful, and his bitterness cut into his heart like a knife. He suppressed the urge to let his eyes linger on the soft white countenance, full lips, and mass of ebony hair, forcing himself to escape after services were over as quickly as possible. As a result, some at church decided Frederic was unfriendly, probably because of the war and his crippled leg. But his family understood. If he left after church in a hurry and started walking, they picked him up along the road on the way home and said nothing.

Plans for Cassie's wedding progressed swiftly and kept the household in a high fever of excitement. Cassie had finished her sewing. Her dresses and underclothing were done and the calico curtains up. She and Bill moved their used pieces of furniture and hand-made items into the cabin. The beautiful four poster had been lovingly finished and placed in the larger bedroom. Ladies at church held a bridal shower, and shelves stood stocked with canned goods, preserves, towels, quilts, bedding, dishes, and cooking pots. The completed cabin stood ready and waiting for the bride and groom.

Frederic avoided visiting the cabin. Each time Cassie asked him to see it, he made an excuse, and his heart tightened up inside. Seeing the little house only reminded him that he too might have had a cabin like it, the one he had planned to build for Becky Sue.

"Please, Fred, just come and see what we've done," Cassie begged one afternoon. "Tell me if you like it or not. . .that's all I ask."

Frederic finally gave in. "I'll come."

The ride was a quiet one as he, Cassie, and Emily took the buggy over to the cabin. Frederic walked through the rooms in silence, his mouth set in a firm line.

"Don't you like it, Fred?" Cassie asked. "Tell me what you're thinking."

"It's a fine cabin, Cassie. It's exactly what I planned to build myself. Bill and his pa did a good job on it. And your curtains. . .well, they're prettier than fair to middlin'."

Cassie hugged her brother. "I'm so glad you like it. I knew you would. Emily doesn't like it a bit."

"I do so, Cassie," Emily sputtered defensively. "I like it a lot, for you and Bill. It's just not what I'd want, that's all."

At that moment a horseman flew up the trail, raising a cloud of dust, and stopped abruptly at the porch. Frederic noted that the rider was a girl, but she was an odd-looking character in faded coveralls a mile too big. Her red-gold hair was formed into a braid that reached to her waist.

"Hello!" a feminine voice shouted as she jumped from her sorrel mare.

"Who is that?" Frederic whispered.

"You know her—that's Bill's sister, Sarah Jane," Cassie replied softly. "Sarah," she called. "Come on in."

"Been out riding and saw your buggy," Sarah said. "Thought maybe Emily and Frederic might be along. Hello there, Frederic." Sarah's smile lit up her small oval face. "I've seen you at church, but you always rush off so fast. I'm glad your leg is okay and that you're home safe."

"Thanks, Sarah, my leg's fine. Well, I wouldn't have recognized you. You've grown taller since I left. You were just a little freckle-faced kid."

"I'm almost fifteen," Sarah declared indignantly. "And I'm the best rider in these parts. I can outride anyone. . .even you, Frederic."

"Well, that's quite a boast. We'll have to see about that," Frederic laughed.

"When, Frederic?" Sarah asked quickly. "When will you ride with me?"

Frederic studied this slip of a girl in her baggy coveralls. She certainly was straightforward and outspoken. Loose wisps of red-gold hair framed her pale delicate face. She gazed at him expectantly with her dark violet-blue eyes, waiting for his answer.

Emily broke the silence. "Sarah's a tomboy, like me. You'd have to ride some to beat her, Fred."

"When can we ride?" Sarah asked again.

Frederic smiled at her persistence. "We'll give it a try one of these days and see who outrides who. I haven't done much riding in the past three years, but I reckon I can outride a little whippersnapper like you."

"Ho. . .just you try!" Sarah declared confidently.

Cassie took Sarah on a tour of the cabin. The younger girl hadn't seen it since it was finished and all the furniture in place.

"It's beautiful, Cassie," Sarah exclaimed. "I knew it would be. Your curtains make it real home-like."

They talked some about the wedding and everyone avoided talking about Becky Sue. Eventually Cassie, Emily, and Frederic climbed into the buggy and headed home.

"Don't forget, Frederic," Sarah called as she hopped on her mare. "We'll race together, you promised. Shall we have a prize for the winner?"

"Yep, and you decide the prize, Sarah. How about cookies? Remember, I'll be the one winning it."

"Don't count your chickens," Sarah shouted as she rode off, her long red-gold braid trailing in the breeze.

seven

Cassie's wedding day, early in September, dawned beautiful and sunny. The hot, humid days were past, and the breeze fresh and invigorating. Trees had started to change color, and a definite promise of autumn filled the air.

Excitement reigned at the Mason household. Ma pressed Pa's and Grandpa's best suits. Frederic purchased a new suit in town, his old pre-war one not being suitable for his sister's wedding. Ma dressed in palest pink, her favorite color that brought out the roses in her cheeks. Emily also wore pink, though a deeper color, with matching bows in her dark brown hair. Cassie and Bill were having only Bill's friend, Peter Jordan, and Emily stand up for them, since they wanted a small wedding. Frederic hoped to stay in the background. He wouldn't miss his sister's wedding for anything, but he wondered how he would avoid Becky Sue.

"I'll just have to grin and bear it," he decided. "Guess I'm not the first man to be thrown over for another by a fickle woman."

Nervously, he dressed and prepared to leave with his parents and grandfather in the larger buggy. Cassie and Emily went ahead in the small buggy with old Nell.

The little church was full of people. Friends and neighbors came in their buggies from miles around. A wedding gave an occasion and excuse to get everyone together for a social gathering. No one wanted to miss it.

Cassie looked beautiful and radiant. Her chestnut hair, pulled back from her face, cascaded into curls around her shoulders. The dress of purest white fit snugly around her tiny waist, then billowed out into layers of ruffles and lace. She had sewn pearl-like beads on the bodice neckline and on the crown of the veil.

Bill stood at the front of the church, nervous but handsome in his dark suit and tie. His hair was plastered down and his blue eyes sparkled. The little lines in his face twitched occasionally as Chase Mason walked his daughter down the aisle to give her away.

Aunt Maude McClough, Pa's widowed sister, sat with the family in the front pew. Medium in height, her slightly rounded figure was draped in lavender and lace. Her dark, snappy eyes commanded attention, and her thick dark hair, streaked heavily with gray, nestled under a perky straw bonnet complete with elegant feathers.

Being ten years older than her brother Chase she tended to be doting and somewhat bossy. Upon hearing about Cassie's upcoming wedding, she spoke out against it. "Fiddlesticks, Chase," she protested loudly. "Cassie is too young. Mark my words, it will never work. Why they are both babes."

Despite her repeated warnings, the young couple continued with their plans. Maude sat, lips pinched together, and fidgeted impatiently with her gloves. Although the wedding did not have her approval, she had presented the couple with a generous gift of money so they could travel to Boston for their honeymoon.

Maude lived comfortably in a large brick home in Waterville near the Common. Her late husband, a doctor for many years, left her well off financially. Having no children of her own, her brother's three children held special places in her heart. She had been allowed the pleasure of showering them with gifts on special occasions through the years.

The pastor of the little church, Rev. Clyde Davis, was a

short, man in his early seventies. He had thin gray hair, a waxed handlebar mustache, and wore thick horn-rimmed spectacles. He spoke the marriage ceremony in a deep, resonant voice and quoted Scripture verses from memory. After the young couple repeated their vows, he admonished them to love one another "till death do you part."

When the marriage ceremony ended, Mrs. Mason was sobbing quietly. Frederic, seated on one side of her, placed a comforting arm about her shoulders. She leaned against him and dabbed at her swollen eyes.

"Now, Ma, don't take on so," her husband whispered from the other side. "Don't let Cassie see ya cryin'. Ya don't want ta spoil it fer her."

"Land-a-goshen," Ma sighed. "Jest look at me, would ya? I'm happy my little girl is married to sech a fine boy. These are jest tears of joy, Pa."

As everyone moved outside, the people gathered around the newlyweds with affectionate hugs and well wishes. Quickly, trestle tables, made of wooden sawhorses and planks, were set up on the grounds and laden with food. Neighbors brought picnic baskets filled with goodies to share in the feast.

Frederic wandered to the back of the property away from the crowd. He sat with his back to the group, surrounded by a small clump of trees. He hoped to be alone and unnoticed in all the excitement. This was Cassie's big day and he wouldn't brood over it. He just wanted to be by himself.

Lost in his own thoughts of self-pity, he was startled by a voice behind him. "Frederic, you've avoided me all these weeks since you came home."

The voice was soft and familiar. Fire rushed to his face as he jumped up and turned to face Becky Sue. Even if he hadn't seen her, he would have recognized her by the delicate sweet scent that met his nostrils.

"Frederic, I've missed you," she continued moving closer. "Remember how it was with us before you went away?"

"Becky Sue!" Frederic's voice sounded strange in his ears, and he caught his breath. "Where's Zack. . .your husband? Isn't he here?"

Becky Sue reached up and touched Frederic's face with her soft hand. "Your mustache makes you look some older, Frederic, but I like it. I like it a lot."

Frederic backed away as though stung. "Where's Zack?" he asked again hoarsely.

"Don't bother about him none, Frederic. He's working all day at the Mill. I made a terrible mistake marrying Zack. I know now that I want us to be like we were before." Becky Sue moved closer and gazed steadily at Frederic. Her sea green eyes held his with a sad and wistful appeal.

Frederic felt himself becoming lightheaded. He shook his head and took a deep breath. "Becky Sue, you are married to Zack," he said firmly. "Things can't be like they were before. We can't go back. God knows I loved you. I planned for three years to come back and marry you. I counted on you waiting for me. You broke your promise as if it meant nothing. You're a married woman, you belong to Zack now. Didn't you hear what the preacher just said? Marriage is 'until death do us part.' That's the way it has to be." He spit out the words and looked away. "Don't you see, it's too late now!"

Frederic turned abruptly and headed back to the festivities. He could hear Becky Sue crying softly, but he didn't turn around. "Don't you see," he muttered to himself bitterly, "it's too late for us now?"

eight

"Over here, Frederic," Emily called from a group of people gathered to one side. "Come join us."

Frederic wanted to be swallowed up in the crowd so he wouldn't have to face Becky Sue again. Quickly, he joined them and greeted many of his old friends, some who were now married. Peter Jordan had a cousin with him, Collette, visiting from Portland. She was small with lots of dark hair and striking black eyes. Her stylish pale yellow dress highlighted the depth of her olive complexion. When introduced, she smiled demurely and held out her hand.

"Nice to meet you," Frederic said.

Time passed quickly as Frederic spent it in lengthy conversation with this interesting and well-educated young lady. Collette spoke French fluently.

"My mother is French," she explained, "and we've been to France many times. I grew up learning the language."

Fascinated at her perfect diction, Frederic found this well traveled miss very enjoyable company, and the distraction welcome. Collette's father was a successful Portland businessman. His shipyard boasted a number of ships involved in the trade market. He had established his headquarters in New Orleans, married her mother there, and until the war, spent winters in New Orleans and summers in Portland. The war had caused heartache and hardship for her family.

"Southerners were naturally suspicious of us," Collette said in her light southern drawl. "This resulted in our moving permanently to our home in Portland for the duration of the war.

Mama and I are so homesick for New Orleans."

"Will your family move back now that the war is over?" Frederic asked.

"Not right away. It may take years to gain confidence with the South, although we have many ties and relatives there. I do so want to go back. My heart has always been in the South."

"How sad that they are suspicious of you. Your family was as much a victim of this war as we soldiers. I have an idea that it will take a little time for all of us."

Frederic learned that Collette would be visiting the Jordans for a few weeks, and requested permission to call upon her.

"Bond's Cornet Band from Boston will be in town next week at the Meeting House. They are well known for their music. Would you go with me?"

"Why, Frederic, it would be a pleasure."

They said their goodbyes and Frederic hurried to help his family clear away food and place wedding gifts in the large buggy. Cassie and Bill had slipped away earlier and caught the train for Boston. They would be gone a week.

Frederic carried an armload of gifts to the Collins' wagon, as they were also transporting gifts to Cassie and Bill's cabin. He was deep in thought about Collette. *Did she notice my crippled leg? She never asked any questions. Probably too polite. I wonder if it matters to her.* As he turned around, he bumped into someone standing directly behind him.

"Sorry, Sarah," he exclaimed. "Where'd you come from?"

"Been right here, Frederic," she laughed.

Frederic hadn't noticed her all afternoon, but all of a sudden here she was. The slender, slip of a girl with reddish-golden hair looked older somehow. Her hair wasn't in a braid today; instead it was tucked and curled about her shoulders for the wedding. *Could she really be only fourteen?* He noted that her soft, misty green muslin dress complimented her fair coloring. *What an improvement over the ridiculous baggy coveralls.*

"Don't be draggin' your feet about riding with me," Sarah Jane reminded.

"Mercy, Sarah, you can't be the same girl I saw at the cabin in baggy britches, can you?" Frederic teased. "I reckon you look a mite older today in that fancy dress."

"I like baggy britches!" Sarah exploded. "Can't ride fast in a dress. When are we taking our ride? You promised, remember?"

Frederic grinned at her impatience. "Things have been busy, Sarah, with the wedding and harvest."

"But will you ride with me sometime?"

"I promised and I will. . .sometime. I can't say when just now."

Frederic thought about the day's events as he and Emily rode home together in the small buggy. Emily chattered constantly about the wedding, the people, and the visitor from Portland.

"Peter's cousin is a real lady, don't you think, Frederic? She's older, twenty-five someone said, and does have some fancy ways. Guess she's bored to death around here."

"Oh, I don't know about that," Fred said thoughtfully.

"What do you think of her? You were talking to her a lot. Is she to your liking?"

"She's very nice. As a matter of fact, we're going to the band concert at the Meeting House on Thursday. We both enjoy good music and she agreed to go."

"Do you think she's pretty?" Emily pressed. "She sure has a lot of dark hair."

Frederic was quiet for a moment. "She's a fine looking woman, even pretty I guess." He looked away, avoiding Emily's gaze. "She's not as pretty as some," he added softly.

Emily suspected Frederic was thinking about Becky Sue, and changed the subject quickly. "Aunt Maudie is anxious to have me live with her while I attend Colby. She gets so lonely in that big house."

"I'll miss you at home. You'll come back weekends, won't you?"

"I won't go until after Christmas when they start the winter term. So I'll be around for a while yet. Don't know about coming home weekends. . .I might have too much studying to do."

"You'll be meeting new fellas and be busier than can be with your social life," Fred teased.

"I know there will be lots going on at the college. I'll like getting involved."

Just then a small buggy came from behind and pulled up beside them on the road. It was Sarah Jane traveling alone and recklessly at a high speed. "Want to race?" she shouted.

"No, Sarah, no!" Frederic yelled. "Slow down! Don't drive so fast! You'll overturn!"

Sarah waved and pulled on ahead. Her red-gold curls had fallen loose and blew carelessly about her shoulders. Frederic and Emily heard her laughing as she left them behind.

"That child needs a good spanking," Frederic said as he pulled old Nell to a slow trot. "She could have caused an accident."

"You know, Fred, she's really not a child anymore. She'll turn fifteen soon."

"Well, what do you think has gotten into her. . .riding up on us like that?"

"I wonder," Emily mused. "I wonder."

•

nine

The day of the Waterville fair arrived. Pa and Grandpa filled the wagon with wood furniture which had been lovingly hand-crafted especially for this event. Frederic had helped them finish the pieces, and now carefully arranged them in the wagon so they would not get broken on the way into town.

Ma and Emily took their quilts, rag rugs, jellies, preserves, and pickles in the buggy. Since the fair lasted all day, the picnic hamper had been filled with food and drink. Cool weather, darkish and damp, threatened, but the sky brightened some as they packed the wagon. Hopes were high.

Grandpa Caleb, though, planned to stay home and nurse his lumbago. The all day affair was hard on the older man.

Still visiting at the Jordans, Collette had told Frederic she would be at the fair. He had enjoyed the band concert with her at the Meeting House and he'd called on her a few times since. Today they would be together again.

"Seems like you and Collette are getting chummy," Emily teased. "Didn't you say she wants you to visit her in Portland?"

"Yep. I'll probably do it. She's a very persuasive person."

"I noticed," Emily laughed. "She seems to have you in a whirl."

"It might be good for me to get away for awhile," Frederic said soberly. "I need to mull things over."

Waterville's fairgrounds bustled with activity. The family quickly set up in an area designated for those with food and craft items to sell. Judges were on hand to judge the best pickles, pies, and other desserts. Ma had entered her blueberry pie and some of her sweet and sour pickles.

At the far end of the area a lean-to shelter was provided for the animals which would be judged. In previous years, before the war, Frederic had entered a calf, steer, or pig. This year the family decided against it. The wood products and canned items would keep them busy enough.

About midday, Collette appeared, dressed in fine blue muslin with a picnic basket on her arm. "Can you leave for a while?" she asked. "I fixed a picnic lunch and we could take it down by the river."

When Frederic hesitated, the family insisted that he go and enjoy himself for a spell. Cassie and Bill had arrived and planned to help for the remainder of the day.

"Go ahead," Ma insisted. "This is your first fair in three years, son. Look around and don't hurry back."

Frederic and Collette found a quiet spot to picnic away from the mingling crowd. Frederic spread a blanket on the deep grass and they relaxed while they ate. Collette had brought fried chicken, rolls and cheese, and some little cakes. They laughed and talked about little things, then strolled around the grounds visiting the various booths.

"Do you like fairs?" Frederic asked. "We have one every year. I've come here since a little boy, as far back as I can remember. Pa used to carry me on his shoulders."

"I like fairs," Collette assured him. "Especially this one. There are so many quaint, homemade items. . .a great variety to choose from."

They approached the contest area and watched as the judges tasted one pie after another. Then they started on the other desserts.

"How can they decide?" Collette asked. "It must be a very difficult decision."

"I'm sure it is," Frederic agreed. "It would be interesting to be one of the judges. I wouldn't mind tasting all those delicious pies."

Collette tilted her dark head and laughed, a sound like tinkling little bells. "You might get sick," she warned, "or fat."

They walked toward the game booths, and stopped at the shooting gallery.

"Would you like a doll, Collette? I'll try my hand at shooting those ducks." Frederic took the gun and started shooting. He hit enough ducks to select a prize for Collette.

"I'd like the stuffed bear, the big brown one," she said. "Fred, you are an excellent marksman. Have you always shot so well?"

"Pa taught me as a boy. It came in handy during the war."

"Tell me about the war."

Frederic turned away. "No, Collette. It was a terrible war. I want to forget about shooting and dying."

"I understand," Collette said quickly, hugging her bear. "Let's go see the animals instead. They should be interesting."

"Right!" Frederic agreed. "Just wish I had one to show today. There'll be a riding contest too."

Frederic steered Collette toward the back lot where the livestock were kept. Judges graded an assortment of ducks, geese, chickens, pigs, cows, lambs, goats, and horses. Collette stopped suddenly short of the shelter, keeping her distance from the animals. Frederic coaxed her to take a closer look.

"You go on ahead, Frederic," she smiled sweetly. "I'm not used to the smell of animals. Most of them, especially the pigs, are so dirty." She wrinkled her nose in disgust. "Take your time, I'll just wait here." She patted her hair and fluffed out her gown, then she pulled her wrap tightly around her shoulders to keep out the chill, dabbing her handkerchief at her nostrils.

Frederic hurried eagerly forward. The animals were like friends to him and he even relished the smell. "Yep," he grinned taking a deep breath, "it just goes with the territory."

He wandered along the stalls until he came to the far end of the shelter where there was a fenced area and several people on horseback. "This has to be the horseback riding contest," he muttered. Just then he noticed a slip of a girl in baggy coveralls astride a sorrel-colored mare. "Can that be Sarah Jane?" he said aloud. "It must be her, with that red hair and baggy britches."

Sarah spied him and rode over. "Frederic! Will you watch while I put Star through her paces? You'll have to come around to the other side."

Frederic nodded and hurried as fast as his bad leg would permit. Standing by the rail, he watched Sarah trot Star out to the center of the ring. Forgetting the time, he watched her entire performance as she trotted, cantered, jumped, and galloped her mare in the competition before the judges.

When finished, Sarah rushed up to him. "How did I do, Frederic? Did I do okay?"

"Better than okay, little one. I'd say you will probably win yourself a ribbon, if I'm any judge."

"Last year I got a third place ribbon. This year I worked harder and I'm older. I'm hoping to get a first place."

Frederic gazed steadily at this youngster in her baggy britches. "Do I look older to you, Frederic?" Sarah searched his face intently with her deep violet-blue eyes. He found it difficult to look away and stood gazing back at her for some time.

"Someone's calling for you, Frederic," Sarah said finally. "It's that fancy French lady from Portland."

Frederic spun around to see Collette walking toward him.

She had a look of determination on her otherwise pretty countenance. Frederic had forgotten her completely. Hurriedly, he said goodbye to Sarah Jane and apologized to Collette.

"I'm sorry, Collette. I got so interested in watching the horseback riding contest."

"Who is that odd child you were talking to?" she asked.

"She's a neighbor," Frederic answered. Then he added thoughtfully, "But she's really not a child."

ten

Autumn's glorious colors blazed across the land. Towering trees with their leaves of gold, yellow, red, and orange painted the countryside. Warm days prevailed, and completion of the harvest was at hand. Nights were cold and crisp, with clear, starry skies overhead.

The men cleaned, repaired, and readied the barn for the animals who spent the long winter inside its walls. Cassie joined the women folk as they did up squash and pumpkins. They made applesauce, apple butter, and jugs of apple cider from an abundance of apples grown in the orchard. The cider filled the air with a delicious aroma that was both tantalizing and inviting. As they completed their canning, they stored the jars on shelves in the pantry or in the cellar under the house.

Cassie took a share of canned products with her to her cabin. Divinely happy in her new role as housewife, her conversation centered around her new husband and their little home. Emily, unable to share in her sister's enthusiasm, grew more and more impatient to start college.

Aunt Maude had generously offered to put up the funds for all of her brother's children so they could receive a college education. She was disappointed that Emily was the only one to take advantage of her offer.

While visiting the farm for dinner one crisp fall Sunday, Maude pressed upon Frederic the importance of higher education. "Frederic," she said in her commanding tone. "You need to get more schooling and make something out of yourself. Farming is all right for your pa and grandpa. They didn't

48

have the opportunity given them for advanced learning. But you, boy, you need something more challenging. Have you no goals? Have you no ambition?" Aunt Maude was known to speak her mind and never very tactfully.

"I do have goals, Aunt Maude. I plan to wrestle the land. As far as more schooling is concerned, no. I'm happy here on the farm. I feel close to my Maker when I'm out in the fields. God speaks to me and we commune together in the beauty of His creation. Yep, everything I want is right here."

"Talk some sense into him, Chase. Do you want to be a farmer all your life, Frederic? Surely you can't be satisfied. . ."

Chase interrupted, "Now, Maude, let the boy alone. He's been away ta the war and seen a lot of terrible things. He's old enough ta know what he wants ta do. Farmin' is a good way ta live. . .Grandpa and I can tell ya. Anyway, it's his life, let the boy decide."

Maude sat tight-lipped for a moment. She didn't take defeat easily. Being outnumbered, however, she resigned herself and added, "If you change your mind, Frederic, just say the word. The funds are there for you." As an afterthought she said, "Are you still seeing the young lady from Portland?"

"I haven't seen her for a few weeks. She's gone back to her family in Portland."

"She invited Fred to visit her," Emily said with a grin.

"Is that so, Frederic?" Aunt Maude asked. "You should go and meet her family. I understand they are important people and quite wealthy."

"I'm thinking on it," Fred answered. "Maybe now is a good time to go with the harvest about done. What do you think, Pa?"

"You've been workin' hard, son, and it'd do ya good ta get away fer awhile. Grandpa and I can carry on here. There's not much ta do right now. We got all the hard stuff done."

"Watch out fer the fancy lady," Grandpa added slyly. "I think she had her eye on our Fred, boy."

Frederic shook his head. "She's a nice friend, Grandpa, that's all. I've enjoyed her company. It kept me from thinking about other things. It'll be just a friendly visit. . .no strings attached. It would be nice to visit Portland."

"That's right, son," Ma agreed. "Jest go, meet her people, and have yerself a good time. Portland is a nice place fer visitin' and ya can stay with cousin Amos and Sophie. They'd be so pleased."

"Now, Frederic," Aunt Maude snapped, "it wouldn't do any harm to think about the possibility of marrying into such a fine well-to-do family. This young woman might be just the one for you."

"She'll press you, Fred," Emily teased. "Collette has marriage on her mind."

A shadow crossed Frederic's brow as he answered. "I'm not ready for a serious relationship. Not now. Maybe never. I'm still not over Becky Sue."

After an awkward silence, Emily said quietly, "Becky Sue has left Zack and is living back home. She wants out of her marriage. . .says it was a mistake."

Frederic muttered an excuse and quickly left the table. He couldn't trust his feelings. Emily's words pounded in his brain: "Becky Sue has left Zack. It was all a mistake." First a glad feeling of hope flooded his being. Then despair washed over him.

He clenched his fists and pounded his injured leg. "It's no good this way," he confessed bitterly, alone in his room. "Please help me, Lord, to win over these feelings I have. I know they're wrong. I need to put Becky Sue out of my mind forever. How can I love someone and hate her at the same time?"

After a fitful night with very little sleep, Frederic arose early and hitched up old Nell to the wagon. He'd wrestled with his painful emotions and made a decision. "Come on, Nell, old girl," he said. "Let's head for town and see if we can get this straightened out. I need to talk to Zack."

The movement of the wagon along the rutted, bumpy, gravel road lulled Frederic into a state of sleepy depression. Fleeting glimpses of Becky Sue and all her loveliness flashed before him, taunting him, teasing him. He could almost hear her speaking.

"I made a mistake marrying Zack, Frederic. I want us to be like we were before." Her soft, inviting words pulled at his heart and he shook his head wildly to rid himself of her face . . .her voice. Memories tortured him. . .of her hand in his as they walked together, the faint scent of her touch as he encircled her waist and drew her close. When they kissed, it was tender and gentle. . .soft as a summer breeze. Becky Sue would laugh and pull away, then look up at him with an impish grin.

"I've got to block out these memories!" Frederic fairly shouted the words. "Becky Sue is married to Zack, and she will never be my wife! I must accept it and try to forget."

Frederic forced himself to repress thoughts of Becky Sue for the remainder of his ride into town. With an anxious heart, he approached the mill shortly before opening time. *Will Zack talk to me? He's probably angry and blames me for Becky Sue's return to her parents. I've got to convince him it's not my idea, and hope he believes me.*

Mr. Turner, Zack's father, was startled to see Frederic so early in the morning. "What can we do fer ya, Fred? Yer pa need some more lumber?"

"Not today, sir. Is Zack around? I'd like to speak to him, if

I may."

"He's inside the office catching up on some paperwork. Go right on in, Fred."

As Frederic entered the small office, he cleared his throat and fumbled for the right words. "Morning, Zack. How are you?"

Zack Turner pushed back a shock of sandy hair as he looked up from his desk of papers. He seemed haggard and sunken-eyed, while his body, always wiry, appeared thinner than usual. "Fred, what can I do for you?" he mumbled. "Do you need more wood?"

"I need to talk to you, Zack. Could you spare me a few minutes?"

"Sure," Zack replied, leaning back in his chair. "Sit down. Is it about Becky Sue? You want her back, don't you?"

Frederic hesitated, then said hurriedly, "No, Zack. . .she's your wife. She belongs with you. I didn't know she'd left you until last evening."

"She's not in love with me. . .never was," Zack muttered bitterly. "She's left me because she's still in love with you."

"Becky Sue might think she's in love with me. She's not . . .or she would never have married you."

"Aren't you glad about this, Fred? Now's your chance to get her back. She only married me because she thought you'd lost your leg. I just happened to be around when she needed someone."

"I'm not happy about this situation one bit," Fred said emphatically. "I loved Becky Sue. . .thought about her every day for three years. But she didn't wait for me. She married you and that's it. Don't you love her, Zack?"

The sandy-haired young man stood up. He looked stricken, tears brimming his eyes. "I love her more than life itself . . .and always will."

"Then go to her," Frederic said firmly, "and ask her to return. Don't wait another day."

Zack brushed the tears away and grasped Frederic's hand. "Thanks, Fred. I'll do just that."

As Frederic headed old Nell back to the farm, he struggled with his inner feelings. "I know it's right that Zack and Becky Sue get back together. That's the way it has to be. But, God, why does it have to hurt so much?"

eleven

The train followed the scenic Kennebec River lined with its magnificent birch trees. Frederic stared thoughtfully out the window, watching the river as it hurried toward the sea. He needed this time to get away for a while. His pa's cousin Amos, a seaman, and his wife Sophie lived in Portland, Maine. Frederic would stay with them for a spell. He'd packed a few belongings, planning to return within the week.

He slumped in his seat, more absorbed in his thoughts than the scenery. The monotonous clickety-clack, clickety-clack, clickety-clack of the train wheels seemed to laugh at him and say, "Becky Sue, Becky Sue, Becky Sue." He struggled unsuccessfully to put her out of his mind.

As the train neared Portland, the harbor town, it bathed in shimmering sunshine, displaying the magnificent granite bulwarks of the coast. The town stood like a sedate lady, surrounded by her jewels, the islands of Casco Bay, bidding a hearty welcome to crafts from many ports. The coast was granite ledges and twisted pines, while roads rambled, dipped, and curved, following this mysterious wonder. Lobstermen and fishermen dotted the harbor in their small dories as they set their twine or baited their trawls.

A short walk from the train station, his cousin's stately old house lay near the harbor. Frederic had visited there many times as a boy, and he loved the salt spray of the air and gray granite coast with its pounding surf. He watched sea birds spread their wings and fly gracefully on their way out to sea.

Sophie and Amos Mason, a warm and homey couple,

greeted Frederic heartily. They welcomed his visit and listened to all the family news from Waterville. Sophie, a small chubby woman with a round face, seemed always to be smiling. Amos, the "old salt," had a tanned, leathery face and large gnarled hands. He owned a fishing boat and made his livelihood from the sea. The raw winds from the sea stiffened his joints, and he hobbled slightly as he showed Frederic to his room, a simple alcove with bed and chest of drawers.

Sophie served a delicious supper of hearty fish chowder, fish cakes, baked beans, and suet pudding. At their request, Frederic related some of his war experiences. Their only son, Samuel, had been killed early in the war at Bull Run. Sadness and pride shone in their eyes as they listened to Fred's stories. He purposely made them brief and minimized the horrors and killing.

With a little encouragement, Amos then related colorful tales of the sea. His stories were endless. With good humor, he spun yarn after yarn late into the night, while they sat around the fireplace.

The next afternoon Frederic called upon Collette. The Jordan home turned out to be a beautiful Victorian mansion. A servant opened the door and ushered him into a large library filled with shelves of various books. The furniture looked imported and was covered with expensive brocade tapestry. Fine pieces of porcelain, from around the world, sat on beautiful carved tables.

When Collette appeared, Frederic was studying the books on the shelves. "Father does have a great collection," she said, holding out her hands to him. "Frederic, I'm so glad you've come."

The fall day was glorious, and the couple spent the afternoon on a tour of Portland. Frederic felt a strange sense of importance as they rode in the fancy carriage with its beautiful thoroughbred horses. The driver handled the horses well along the rambling, curving roads that followed the sea. They stopped briefly at the cousins' so Frederic could tell them he would be having dinner with the Jordans.

Sophie and Amos made a fuss over Collette and offered her some tea and cakes.

"Oh, no, thank you," she said curtly. "We must be getting home."

As they headed toward the Jordan home in the carriage, Collette commented on the simpleness of the cousins' home. "Your father's cousins are so quaint. Is fishing all he does for a living?"

"They're rare down-home folk," Frederic said defensively. "The best. I've always loved visiting Pa's cousins by the sea. If I wasn't a farmer, I would probably turn to the sea."

Dinner at the Jordans was a lavish and delicious meal served in the formal dining room. Frederic felt ill at ease, but his host and hostess received him warmly. Mrs. Jordan was another Collette, only older and heavier. Mr. Jordan, tall with a lean, angular jaw, had a firm mouth and keen, observant eyes. He talked at great length about his shipbuilding business, the cargo trade from port to port, and his desire for a young man to learn the business. His talk centered only upon his work, and Frederic suspected that it consumed his entire life. Frederic listened politely and after a length of time realized that, for some strange reason, Mr. Jordan was hinting that Frederic might be the "young man" he was looking for.

ॐ

In the days that followed Frederic and Collette walked or rode around the scenic spots of Portland. Mr. Jordan insisted on showing Frederic his buildings and offices located near the harbor. He seemed determined Frederic would consider a position with him.

"Mr. Jordan, I appreciate your confidence in me. But I'm a farmer. I know nothing about the trade business."

"I'll teach you," Mr. Jordan said forcefully. "You can learn it just as I did."

The pressure made Frederic uncomfortable and he welcomed an escape with Collette to walk along the sea. They watched the fog roll in and enshroud them like a heavy mantle. They laughed when the deep blue of the pounding surf caused the salt spray to sting their faces. They saw the large boats come in and listened to the tolling of the bell buoys, and then slowly they walked back toward town.

Later that night, Frederic shared with Sophie and Amos his hurt and bitterness over Becky Sue and also Mr. Jordan's offer of a position. In their kind way they offered words of wisdom.

"God will mend yer heart," Sophie said. "Ya jest have ta give it over ta Him completely. Time heals. God allows these things ta happen fer a purpose."

Amos gave him words of warning about the position with Mr. Jordan. "Don't be acceptin' it jest because it means a lot of money. If yer heart's not in the work, don't do it. Money isn't that important. God gives us a choice as ta how we're ta make our livin'. Me, I chose fishin' and the sea. Freddy, yer a farmer. Ya say ya love workin' the soil. Then do it. Don't let anyone change yer mind."

Frederic felt better after their talk. They had given simple and direct counsel which spoke to his heart.

The week, so enjoyable at times, passed quickly. His last evening with the Jordans he told them his goodbyes.

"There is a fine opportunity waiting for you, young man, in my shipping business. I need someone like you, enthusiastic, enterprising, with a fine head on his shoulders." Mr. Jordan extended his hand as he spoke. "I'll pay you well. It's an offer of a lifetime, so give it serious thought."

"Yes, sir, I will think about it. It's a very tempting offer although I don't think I'm suited to an office job."

"Goodbye then," Mr. Jordan said curtly. "Let me know your decision as soon as possible."

Collette walked Frederic to the door. "You must accept his offer, Frederic. It would give me so much pleasure. We could be together all the time."

Frederic looked into her dark pleading eyes. *Were there strings attached to the job?*

"I'll think about it, Collette," he said. "But I can't promise anything."

twelve

Frederic walked swiftly in the brisk night air to his cousins' home by the sea. He was grateful to find Amos still up, reading quietly by the fire.

"Ah, lad. . .so soon ya have to leave us, eh?" the older man said. "We'll miss ya when ya go."

"And I'll miss you and Sophie, cousin Amos. You've been so gracious, I feel right at home here. And I've appreciated your advice about Mr. Jordan's offer."

Amos stared into the fire for some time before answering. "Ah, Jordan is a keen and shrewd businessman, that he is. He's amassed a fortune in a way that, according to rumor, was not allus on the fair and square. I jest say. . .don't be hasty, lad. We Mason menfolk have allus been men o' the sea or men o' the soil. I'm not sayin', mind ya, thet ya can't break out o' the mold. I'm jest sayin' ta ponder it slow-like and search this Book fer yer answer." Amos handed Frederic his worn Bible and bade him good night.

Frederic read Amos' Bible late into the night. This was something he'd neglected for a long time. He remembered Isaiah 26:3 from memory. "Thou wilt keep him in perfect peace, whose mind is stayed on thee because he trusteth in thee."

"I haven't been trusting," he muttered. "That's why I haven't had any peace. Forgive me, Lord."

As he read and meditated on God's Word, Psalm 61 spoke to his heart. "Hear my cry, O God; attend unto my prayer. From the end of the earth will I cry unto thee, when my heart is overwhelmed: lead me to the rock that is higher than I."

Then and there he turned his broken heart over to God and left it with Him. A feeling of peace settled over Frederic. His bitterness toward Becky Sue vanished. . .and he realized he didn't love her anymore, nor did he hate her. "Thank you, God," he whispered.

Frederic enjoyed the train ride home. He had gone to Portland depressed and with a heavy heart; he came away contented and at peace with God. The prospect of a new job with a bright future entered his thoughts.

Could I refuse such an offer? Mr. Jordan made it clear that he wanted me for the position. Why would he want me? I'm just a farm boy. Of course it's Collette. She probably begged her pa to give me a job. She almost insisted that I take it. Amos is right. . .I need to give it a great deal of thought.

෴

Back home the family listened eagerly about his visit with Sophie and Amos. Frederic recited his good times with the cousins and how he and Collette enjoyed touring Portland each day. His family were impressed when he went into great detail describing the Jordan mansion, the fine furniture, expensive brocade tapestries, and exquisite china. He mentioned Mr. Jordan's offer of a good position in his shipbuilding business. "He pressed me about taking it at every opportunity."

"Yep, the wheel thet squeaks the loudest gets the grease," Pa reasoned. "What did ya tell him, son?"

"I told him I'd think on it. Collette most likely put her pa up to it."

"What's he got in mind?" Grandpa asked. "A husband fer his daughter, maybe?"

"I wondered about that, Grandpa. Nothing was said, of course."

"But that's on Collette's mind, you can bet," Emily said wrinkling her nose. "She's after you, Frederic."

"Son, ya might be leavin' us fer a job in Portland?" Ma's voice showed her disappointment. "Why, we jest got ya back home again."

"I'm to think on it, Ma, that's all. There's no decision yet."

"Be sure ya pray about it, son," Pa stated. "None of us want ya ta go, unless it's God's will."

&

The next week Frederic called on Becky Sue. She was still with her parents, separated from Zack. Fred knew he could handle seeing her now that God had changed his attitudes. He still cared for her as a friend, and was concerned about her future. He'd hoped his talk with Zack would bring the couple back together.

"Evidently Becky Sue is being stubborn," he murmured. "Guess she needs to hear it from me. If I talk to her, maybe I can convince her to return to her husband. Zack still loves her and wants her. She must know that. God made them one, and they belong together."

Fred knocked on the old wooden door, cleared his throat, and heard footsteps approaching. He swallowed hard, ready to face Becky Sue.

Mrs. Collins, wiping her hands on her checked apron, seemed surprised to see him. "Frederic!" she exclaimed. "How nice of you to call."

"Hello, Mrs. Collins. Is Becky Sue at home? I'd like to talk to her if it's a convenient time."

"Of course, Frederic. Come on into the parlor and I'll get Becky Sue. She mopes around the house a lot these days. It will do her good to see you. I'm sure it will lift her spirits."

Frederic paced back and forth as he waited for Becky Sue. *Lord, help me say the right words. Help me get these two back together. They need one another. I know that's what You want, too.*

Becky Sue burst into the room and ran toward him. "Frederic! I knew you'd come. I just knew it!" Her face glowed with color and her eyes sparkled like shining green jewels.

"I came to talk to you, Becky Sue, as a friend," Frederic explained. "Can we talk a spell?"

Becky Sue took his arm and pulled him toward the sofa. "Let's sit down, Fred, it's so much cozier. And yes, we have lots to talk about, don't we?"

Fred disentangled her arms and settled himself some distance from her. He noticed her delicate ivory coloring, the slight lift of her chin, and her full wistful lips. *She's as beautiful as ever,* he thought. *But she's acting like a spoiled child.*

"Becky Sue, I talked to Zack a while back."

"I know about your conversation, Fred. What about it?"

"He wants you to come back. He's your husband and that's where you belong."

"Why?" Becky Sue pouted. "I love you and you love me. That's all that matters."

"No, it isn't, Becky Sue. I did love you, yes. But not any more."

Becky Sue moved closer on the sofa and touched Fred's face with her soft hand. Her eyes searched his. "You do love me, Fred. You promised you always would. I remember your promise."

Frederic cleared his throat. "I did promise you that three years ago. I loved you and you promised to wait for me until after the war. You broke your promise, Becky Sue, and that nullifies mine."

Becky Sue smiled up at him with her sweetest smile. "But that can be changed, Fred. I made a mistake marrying Zack. It was a terrible mistake, I know. Don't you understand? I can get out of this marriage and we can be sweethearts again. You must know I don't love Zack. . .I only love you."

"No, you only think you love me. It was a long time ago and we were young and in love. When I first came home, I thought I'd never get over loving you. Yes, I loved you, Becky Sue, but I almost hated you for what you'd done. God showed me how wrong I was to have such bitter feelings. He rescued me from the pit of bitterness and now we can be friends. I'd like that."

"I don't want to be just friends," Becky Sue sputtered. "Don't you remember all the good times we had. . .the quiet walks. . .the picnics. . .how can I forget everything we meant to each other?"

"God wants to help you, just as He did me. He'll help you love Zack. He takes our mistakes and works things for our good. He does it all the time. Go back to Zack and be a good wife to him. He loves you very much. I know God will help you learn to love him. Please, Becky Sue. Will you at least try?"

Becky Sue was crying softly. "I'll try, Frederic, if that's what you want."

"It's what God wants. That's what's important. We need to do His will. He can't bless us when we disobey His Word." Fred patted her arm and stood up. "I'll be praying for you," he whispered. "Everything will turn out fine, you'll see."

Frederic slipped out the kitchen door and heaved a sigh of relief. He felt like a heavy load had just been lifted from his shoulders. Becky Sue had agreed to go back to Zack and be his wife. "It will work out for them," he muttered, "if they both let God rule their hearts and their home."

Fred almost bumped into Sarah as she came in from the barn. She was dressed in her usual baggy britches and her red-gold hair was tousled and windblown.

"Frederic!" she exclaimed in delight. "Did you come to ride? It's a fine day for it."

"Not today, Sarah. I've been visiting Becky Sue. We had some things to talk over."

Sarah's face clouded. "She's still married to Zack, you know. They're only separated."

"Yep, I know. That's what we talked about. I told her to go back to him. That's where she belongs. . .with her husband. Zack still loves her and wants her to return. They can work their problems out and put their marriage back together."

"Do you mean it? But she keeps talking about you two getting back together, like you are still in love. Are you?"

"It's over, Sarah. I've told her and she knows it now. We are just friends, and that's the way it should be. God can help her love Zack. She thinks she doesn't love him, but God will help her if she'll let Him."

"You don't love Becky Sue!" Sarah said the words aloud as if to convince herself. "Do you love the fancy lady from Portland, then?"

"Collette? She's a nice lady, but she's just a good friend. I'm not in love with anyone right now. I don't expect I will be for a long while." Frederic turned, waved goodbye, and left abruptly.

Questions haunted him as he set out for home. *Could anyone ever replace Becky Sue in his life? Would he ever love again?* The idea seemed impossible, and he shut it out of his mind.

But Sarah entered the house smiling, with a spring in her step and a song in her heart.

thirteen

The first two weeks of November were unusually warm and hazy, an Indian summer to finish the harvest and prepare for the long, black evenings of winter. Winters could be raw and cold with nor'easters blowing in storms and eventually mounds of beautiful white snow.

When Frederic learned Becky Sue had returned to her husband, he was grateful. He wanted things to go well for the young couple and for the marriage to survive. His talk with Becky Sue had proved easier than he had expected. "She knew she belonged with Zack," he muttered. "I only helped her make up her mind."

Collette wrote letters pressuring Frederic to accept her father's business proposition. Dwelling on the beauty of Portland, she reminded him how much they enjoyed being together during his visit. "Wouldn't it be wonderful to have these good times continue? Certainly farming doesn't compare with becoming a city gentleman? Life in Portland could be so exciting if only you were here at my side."

Mr. Jordan sent one brief, terse note outlining the job and suggesting a generous salary. He intimated his offer to be something only a fool would pass up. The letter concluded saying he needed his answer by the first of the year.

Frederic, in a quandary, carried out his chores in a daze. He weighed the reasons for going against the reasons for staying on the farm. His family left him to piece out his own thoughts. Much as his pa wanted him to stay and eventually take over the farm, he knew what a tremendous opportunity his son faced. "Ya must make yer own decision, son," he counseled. "Ya are not beholden ta anyone. Let God be yer Guide."

Frederic reasoned he would make a large amount of money at Mr. Jordan's shipyard. He could give generously toward the needs of the farm. *But would I be happy? Money. . .is that what it's all about? I'd be giving up the farm, the land that I love, the animals, the fresh, pure air in God's great outdoors. For what? An office job, to sit at a desk every day surrounded by four walls.*

The thought stifled him. "How could I stand being cooped up day after day inside? But still, there's good things in favor of the job besides the money. It would be easier on my crippled leg. Much easier. I would sit instead of plow, hoe, cut wood, and do all the other duties involved with farming. But I'd be a traitor, wouldn't I?" he whispered alone in the open field. "I'd be a traitor to all I believe in."

The pure, crisp air caressed his cheeks as he dug his hands deeply into the dirt and let it trickle through his fingers. "This soil, this ground is my life's work, same as pa's and grandpa's. God, I feel Your presence here."

ð

Frederic remembered his promise to Sarah Jane to ride with her. He had postponed the ride many times, but since a promise must be kept, he arranged to meet her and ride before the snow fell.

A bright mid-November afternoon they met on a ridge high on a knoll between the family properties. Riding was awkward for Frederic, since one stirrup had to be shorter than the other to accommodate his shorter leg. "I feel like a beginner, Sarah Jane," he laughed. "You'll probably leave me far behind in your dust."

"Where's your fightin' spirit?" she chided. "You sounded mighty cocky and sure of yourself earlier."

"Well, I'll give it my best shot, and then some. Let's race to my place and may the best man win!"

Frederic nudged Torch, his favorite buckskin, and started off ahead galloping across the field. He breathed deeply, letting the cold, crisp air fill his lungs, feeling exhilarated. He and Torch seemed glued as one unit. . .moving together smoothly and with perfect ease.

Sarah Jane was right beside him on Star, her long braid trailing in the wind. She rode fast, sure of herself. They were neck and neck all the way. A trail through the woods led them to the creek, and finally into the back pasture heading toward the house.

"A tie!" Sarah shouted breathlessly as she jumped from her mare.

Frederic took longer to dismount. "A tie," he agreed. "But next time, I'll win."

Sarah heard the words "next time," and happiness washed over her. They tied the horses to the hitching post and went inside for cider and molasses doughnuts.

As the two riders entered the house, they found Mrs. Mason bustling about the kitchen preparing for the evening meal. "My, the two of ya look like ya could use some warmin' up. Yer cheeks are as rosy as can be. Did ya have a good ride?"

"Oh, yes," Sarah exclaimed. "Fred almost beat me."

"Ma, she can really handle a horse," Fred added. "She sure gave me a hard run, but I managed to keep up with her. . .and like she said, almost beat her, too. Torch never let me down."

"Just set ya down at the table and I'll get the cider and doughnuts. Ya must be hungry after sech a long ride. The air is sharp taday."

Fred and Sarah pulled off their warm jackets and settled themselves at the kitchen table. Mrs. Mason heated the cider and served it with a plate of her homemade doughnuts.

"This will warm ya up," she said placing the mugs before them. "Now eat and enjoy."

"Thanks, Mrs. Mason," Sarah replied. "That air did have a chill to it."

"Thanks, Ma," Fred said. "You always know just what a body needs."

Sarah chattered about school. "It's my last year and I can't wait to graduate in the spring. That's enough schooling for me. The boys are all so childish and full of mischief. Last month they tipped over the outhouse. Miss Ragsdale was so mad!" she laughed.

Her laugh was infectious and Frederic laughed with her, feeling more relaxed than he had in a long time.

"I'm glad you kept your promise about riding with me, Fred. Didn't it seem good to ride again? I'm sure you've been missing it."

"I'd forgotten how good it was, Sarah," he said soberly. "I always loved to ride. I guess I thought this ole leg of mine would limit my riding."

"It didn't hurt you none at all, Fred. You fairly flew along on Torch."

"Well, I feel honored that a nice young girl like you wanted to ride with me."

"And why wouldn't I want to ride with you?"

"I'm just an old crippled soldier from the war, that's why. Sometimes it matters to people."

"You're not old. . .and you're not crippled!" Sarah said emphatically. "And it doesn't matter. . .it doesn't matter at all."

"What do you call this then?" Fred asked, thumping his lame leg. "It's not the same as it used to be."

"Now, Freddy, ya hush," Mrs. Mason interjected. "Yer leg

was hurt in the war, but don't call yerself a cripple jest 'cause ya limp a little. If ya refer ta yerself that a way, ya'll allus feel sorry fer yerself. Ya don't want that."

"No, I don't, Ma. You're right."

"Fred," Sarah said, "you'll carry that limp the rest of your life, as a reminder. Everyone knows our nation went through a terrible war. . .and you were part of it. You fought bravely, were willing to die even, to keep our country united as one and assure freedom from slavery. Remember what President Lincoln said when they dedicated the battlefield at Gettysburg? He said our nation was 'Conceived in liberty and dedicated to the proposition that all men are created equal.' Not one soldier was injured or died in vain. Your injury is really a symbol of honor. I think you should be proud of your limp and how you received it. I am." Sarah sat back, out of breath.

"Sarah Jane, you amaze me. For a youngster of fourteen you seem to have a good head on your shoulders. Do you know Mr. Lincoln's entire Gettysburg Address?"

"Yes I do. Miss Ragsdale made us learn it and recite it in class as part of our grade. And Frederic, I'm fifteen now . . .not fourteen. Just turned last week."

"Well, happy birthday, Sarah Jane," Mrs. Mason said. "Seems like only yesterday ya were jest a little tot. Yer growin' up so fast."

"When I turned twenty-two in September, I felt a lot older," Fred added. "Guess it was because of the war. Those were kind words you said, Sarah, and I appreciate them. I was proud to serve my country and I'm thankful I could. The memories haunt me sometimes, but it's getting easier all the time. It was a war that had to be fought. There was no other way."

Emily came into the kitchen. "Hi, Sarah. You and Fred been riding?" She held out an armful of dress material. "Ma, I have some questions about this dress I'm making. Do you have the time?"

"Jest as soon as I put this apple pie in the oven I'll come up and give ya a hand," Mrs. Mason answered.

"Hello, Emily," Sarah said. "Fred and I had a good ride, and he didn't beat me."

"It was a tie all the way," Frederic stated. "But she's a fast rider and it would be hard to beat her."

"Sarah, come with me upstairs and see the dresses I've sewed for college. I'm so excited about starting in January."

"She's anxious to get away from us," Fred chuckled. "With all her higher schooling, soon she won't want to associate with us peasants."

"Fred, you tease!" Emily gave him a clout on the back. "You know that's not true. Come, Sarah, let's leave this badgerer to himself."

Emily had several dresses, all completed, laid out on her bed. "That's a heap of fancy dresses," Sarah said, impressed. "When will you ever wear that many?"

"We have classes every day and there are social activities. I'll need many different outfits. Aunt Maude is particular. She wants me to dress well. And I enjoy sewing."

"Fancy dresses are such a bother. I'd rather wear these old riding britches any time. Can't ride horses in those kind of get-ups."

"I enjoy riding just as you do. But sometimes it's nice to be a lady, Sarah. A fancy dress and hair-do might catch the eye of a certain fella. That is," Emily whispered mysteriously, "if you're interested."

Sarah Jane's face turned brick red from her hairline down to her throat. With a quick excuse, she ran downstairs and hurried outside.

Frederic called to her as she unhitched Star. "Wait, Sarah Jane, I'll ride home with you. Now that I've ridden Torch once, I see what I've been missing. Let's take our time and mosey on slow-like. I like to take it all in."

Sarah smiled her agreement and climbed on Star. She hoped her face wasn't still flushed. The afternoon had been so perfect and she didn't want it to end. She glanced sideways at Frederic and felt her heart beating wildly.

Emily watched them from the upstairs window as they trotted side by side toward the back pasture. "Sarah's in love with him all right. It's as plain as the nose on her face."

fourteen

The latter part of November brought the snow, sifting down into the quiet, silent woods. It fell softly on the stone walls and fences, covering the evergreens until they bowed down with large puffs of fluffy white.

The Reverend Davis, in his seveties, decided to retire. He and his wife Lucy planned to stay until the new preacher arrived around Thanksgiving. Folks had grown so accustomed to the Davises, that they dreaded to make a change. After all, the Davises had been with them for many years.

The church held a farewell "pounding" for them. The members brought staples of all kinds of canned meats and vegetables for the couple. The pastor's salary had been meager, though sufficient, and augmented through the years with "poundings" on a regular basis.

The new pastor, Robert Harris, was a twenty-two-year-old coming to them fresh out of seminary. The members of the church had mixed feelings about his capabilities. Many resented the fact this would be his first pastorate. Would he be able to fill Pastor Davis' shoes? The young pastor had no wife to play the piano, head up the Ladies' Mission Group, and care for the parsonage.

The members decided since the new pastor was single, he would board with Deacon and Mrs. Meade. They lived near the church on Silver Street, and Mrs. Meade could take the young pastor under her wing. The parsonage would be closed temporarily until the young pastor married.

❧

Robert Harris, a tall slender young man with sandy-colored hair and green eyes, arrived a few days ahead of schedule. Not wanting to inconvenience anyone, he went directly to the Elmwood Hotel on College Street. He planned to stay there until the time expected by the congregation. This would give him time to get familiar with the town and feel at home. He felt excited, yet nervous, about his new pastorate.

He had no family except the grandmother who raised him, and she had recently passed away. While attending seminary, he had worked to support her, and he had missed enlisting in the war because she had needed him.

Waterville would be his town now, he reasoned. Now that his grandmother was gone, these people would be his people, the church congregation his family.

After unpacking his few belongings, he left the hotel and walked briskly south along Main Street from the Common to Ticonic Row. He crossed over the Kennebec River through the covered bridge and passed Lockwood Saw Mill located below the Ticonic Falls. Circling back, he headed north on Main Street and wandered down several other streets: Elm, Pleasant, Water, and Silver. He noticed the home of Mr. and Mrs. Meade on Silver Street and decided, on an impulse, to greet them and let them know he had arrived earlier than planned.

The middle-aged couple greeted him warmly and urged him to move out of the Elmwood Hotel and in with them immediately. He declined until the morrow, but agreed to have supper with them. His brisk walk all over town had left him with a ravenous appetite.

During the supper meal, the Meades told him of news about the church and its people. They were pleased to see the young preacher with such a good appetite and urged him to refill his plate.

"This is fine cooking, Mrs. Meade. I haven't eaten this well since my grandmother died three months ago. She was very dear to me." He told how his grandmother had raised him after his parents died in an accident when he was three. As far as he knew, he had no other relatives.

"You poor boy!" Mrs. Meade exclaimed. "No family. . .no one at all!"

"Well," Robert smiled, "I hope to make Waterville my home and the church folks here my family."

"We do tend to be like one big family at church, don't we dear?" Mrs. Meade looked at her husband.

"Most of the time," Deacon Meade agreed. "But it will take some time for everyone to accept such a young and handsome preacher. Give us time, Robert. Many are hard-nosed and set in their ways, even though changes can be good."

"I plan to try very hard. It's important to me that this work out."

"Don't try too hard, son," Mr. Meade cautioned. "Just be yourself and preach the Word. That's all we ask."

"I will, sir. I'm anxious to get started. Will Pastor Davis still be here on Sunday?"

"Yes, for the morning service. He and his wife plan to leave in the afternoon. Pastor Davis will give you any help he can. Why don't you call on them before Sunday and get some counsel firsthand?"

"I'll do that tomorrow as soon as I've settled in here."

Robert thanked the Meades and left soon after supper. He needed a quiet time back in his room for study before bedtime.

As he walked slowly back to the hotel, the streets had a soft glow, lighted by kerosene lamps. All was quiet except the occasional clip-clop of a passing horse and carriage. Snow fell in large flakes that sparkled under the glow of the lamps.

Soon his coat and hat were covered with the glittering flakes. The air was cold, but he had a warm feeling inside his heart.

"This town has charmed me already," he whispered. "Waterville, I'm home!"

fifteen

Ma and Emily gave the house "a lick and a promise," aired quilts and bedding, and started their baking for Thanksgiving. The menfolk cut timber in the woods and hauled it to the house to be cut in lengths for the fireplaces and wood stove.

The day before Thanksgiving the men loaded the wagon for a trip to the saw mill. Emily decided to go along and do some shopping. She dressed warmly to protect herself against the cold November chill.

Once in town, the men left her at the Common while they went on to the mill. She planned to shop and then go to Aunt Maude's to be picked up later on their way home. The day was bright and sunny, with just enough snow on the ground to make it slippery in spots.

Emily purchased a warm hat, some needed staples, knitting supplies, and another length of yard goods. Overloaded with packages, she didn't notice a patch of ice as she came out of Miller's store and started down the street. In an instant, her feet flew from under her, tossing packages into the air. Feeling clumsy and embarrassed, she found herself sprawled awkwardly on the ground. A young man came quickly to her assistance.

"Let me help you, miss," Robert Harris said, smiling. Without waiting for an answer, two strong arms pulled her to her feet. The young man's eyes met hers and held for a long moment.

Emily looked away, shook herself free, and began brushing snow from her coat. "Thank you," she said stiffly, high spots of color rising on her cheeks.

Robert chuckled and began gathering her packages which had slid every which way. Emily grabbed them from him. "Don't trouble yourself," she said coldly. "I can manage perfectly well."

"It's no trouble, miss," Robert insisted. "Let me carry your packages home for you. You have quite a bundle there."

He reached to take them, but Emily drew back. "No!" she said firmly. "I don't need your help."

He was still smiling at her, a wide, crooked grin that brightened his entire face.

Is he laughing at me? I must have looked foolish and ridiculous sprawled on the ground in such an unladylike fashion.

"It would be my pleasure to carry them," he said.

"I'm only going around the corner to my aunt's house!" she said haughtily. "I don't need any help." She lifted her head, turned, and walked quickly away.

As she rounded the corner, she glanced back. He stood watching her with that silly grin on his face. "Let him laugh," Emily muttered. "I hope I never see him again."

Later, on the way home, Frederic noticed that Emily, usually so talkative, was quiet and deep in thought.

How shameful to fall in public, and be helped by a handsome young man, she was thinking. *He is handsome, even with that crooked smile glued to his face. Well, I won't give him a chance to laugh at me again!*

"I talked with Zack today," Frederic said, trying to draw her out of her silence. He leaned back against the pile of pine boards stacked in the wagon bed. "He works at the mill, you know."

"Umm. . .yes." Emily's voice was absent-minded.

"Well, he and Becky Sue are getting on fine. I told him it

made me happy they are together again. He seemed glad I said that. We've always been good friends, so I guess everything is all right between us."

Emily snuggled closer to her brother to keep out the cold. "I'm glad things worked out so well. . .for all of you."

They were quiet the rest of the way home, lost in their own thoughts. In the front of the wagon, Pa and Grandpa kept up a steady stream of chatter which blended with the rhythmical clip-clop of the team on the hard packed road leading home.

❧

Thanksgiving arrived, the special day set aside by President Lincoln for giving thanks to God for His bountiful blessings. Ma prepared a large turkey complete with stuffing. The squash and mince pies and suet pudding stood in a row on the sideboard, waiting to be devoured. Emily set the table, then played the piano while waiting for Cassie and Bill. The young couple had offered to pick up Aunt Maude in town and bring her out for the feast.

Upon arriving, Aunt Maude bustled into the farmhouse as quickly as her stout legs could carry her. She bubbled with excitement as she greeted each of the family. Quickly, she undid her wool wrap and warm hat and handed them to Emily.

"Frederic!" she exploded. "Frederic, do you know that Miss Jordan is coming to town? Well, of course you do. I heard from my friend Bessie that she'll be here in two weeks and stay through the Christmas holidays." Aunt Maude sat down heavily, flushed and out of breath.

"Yep, Aunt Maude. She wrote she was coming."

"Well, I must say you don't sound a bit excited. What is the matter with you, boy? I'd expect you'd be proud to have a fine lady like Miss Jordan wanting to see you. And she's wealthy too. Bessie says it's common knowledge you and Miss Jordan are practically engaged and you are taking a position in her father's company."

"Whoa, Aunt Maudie!" Frederic exclaimed hastily. "There is no engagement. As for the job, I'm still thinking on it."

"What's to think about?" Aunt Maude insisted. "You can't turn down the offer of a lifetime! Think how important you'd be! Think of the money!"

Aunt Maude's outburst unsettled everyone. A hush fell over the room and every eye turned toward Frederic. He faced his aunt and said softly, "Life doesn't consist in the abundance of things. . .or even money, Aunt Maudie. I'm praying about the job. But when I make my decision, it will be based on how God directs."

sixteen

Emily walked into the church the following Sunday and went straight to the piano. When Reverend and Mrs. Davis left, Emily would take Mrs. Davis' place as the church pianist. Emily flipped through the hymnal, pausing at one of her favorite songs as she began to play softly while she waited for Mrs. Davis to arrive.

"Mighty nice playing," a half-familiar voice spoke in back of her. "Are you the regular pianist—I hope?"

Emily whirled around to face Robert Harris, the same young man who had helped her up after her disgraceful fall. Color once again flamed in her cheeks as he stared at her with the same crooked grin.

"Yes," she stammered. "Or rather, I will be after the Davises leave. Mrs. Davis will play today. And you are. . .?"

"I'm sorry. I'm Robert Harris, the new pastor."

Emily looked aghast, and said nothing.

"Is it that bad?" he questioned, still with a grin on his face.

"No. . .I mean. . .I didn't think. . .I mean," she faltered.

"I see. You didn't think I could be a preacher, is that it?" he teased. "And may I know to whom I have the pleasure of speaking?"

Emily felt like a trapped animal. The church was beginning to fill with people, though, and she could not escape. Strange feelings filled her as her eyes met the steady green eyes of Robert Harris.

"I'm Miss Mason," she answered coolly, rising from the piano. She turned abruptly and walked away.

The church service that morning touched hearts. Rev. Davis reminisced about his many years with the congregation. "We've had times of joy and times of sorrow. You are a good people. Lucy and I have been blessed as we labored here— but it's time for us to move on and turn the reins over to a younger man. We hope you will support Robert Harris as he leads the flock from today on. Come up here, Robert, and tell the folks a little about yourself."

Robert Harris talked about his background and his plans for the future. "I look forward to serving as your pastor," he said. "Please feel free to come to me with any problems or suggestions. I welcome your help. I pray we can work together in a unity of the Spirit."

The congregation formed a line, bidding farewell to the Davises and welcoming Robert Harris at the same time. The Mason family, complete with Grandpa and Aunt Maude, took their places in the line.

Emily could not avoid shaking hands with Robert Harris. He had a firm but gentle handshake and said warmly, "I'm so pleased to make your acquaintance, Miss Mason. I look forward to hearing you play the piano each Sunday."

Emily nodded and moved away. *There is something about those eyes. And that grin. . .crooked and teasing. Is he laughing at me underneath that polished exterior? Is he remembering my unladylike sprawl on the icy ground? Can I never get away from the silly grin?*

The family talked of nothing but the new preacher over dinner. Everyone liked the young man.

"We haven't heard him preach yet, but I think he'll be a good un," Grandpa stated. "He sounds like he aims to please."

"We know he believes as we do. . .it was all in his statement of faith," Pa agreed. "His schoolin' background is good. It'll take us some time though ta get used ta such a young fella."

Ma, Frederic, Bill, Cassie, and even Aunt Maude had only good things to say about the young Reverend Harris.

"He looks like a young man with backbone," Aunt Maude said. "I look forward to his preaching."

"Rev. Davis is a wise man," Pa said. "He knew when it was time fer him ta move on. At his age he needs a rest from all the responsibilities of a church. He's been our pastor fer a long time."

"I'll really miss Lucy," Ma added. "She's been sech a blessin' ta the ladies. She was sech a gracious person and did so many kind things. Young Rev. Harris will need a good wife ta share in his ministry. Course he's young and probably in no hurry. But I hope he gets one ta match Lucy Davis, when he does take a wife."

"Now don't ya go tryin' ta get him married off, Ma," Pa cautioned. "He needs ta get settled in first and get ta know the church folk. It might take a while fer some of our people ta accept the new preacher."

Grandpa reached for seconds on the mashed potatoes. "Who knows, this young feller might have a special lady. . .back where he came from. Did ya ever think of that?"

"Well, he never mentioned it in his get-acquainted talk today," Maude said. "He told us he doesn't have any family . . .none at all. If he had a special lady friend, it seems he would have commented on it. He's probably been so busy with his schooling he hasn't had time for courting."

"I think it will be good for the young people to have a young pastor-leader as a role model. . .someone to look up to," Frederic reasoned. "They haven't had that in Rev. Davis, although he was interested in them and a dear man of God. The young people will relate better and share problems easier with a younger man."

"He's really taken you all in, hasn't he?" Emily asked.

"Well, not me!"

"Don't you like him?" Cassie asked. "I saw you talking to him by the piano before church. Did he make a bad impression?"

"Did he say anythin' out o' the way ta ya, Emily?" Pa asked quickly. "I want ta know if he's not been a gentleman."

"Oh no, he's the perfect gentleman," Emily answered sarcastically. "It's just those searching green eyes of his and that silly crooked grin."

"Aha!" Frederic laughed. "So that's it. You've noticed his eyes and his smile. I suspect you like him a whole lot better than you think."

Emily felt the color rush into her cheeks. "Oh, fiddle!" she exclaimed, jumping up from the table. "I wish I never had to see him again!"

seventeen

With the holidays fast approaching, Emily saw more and more of Robert Harris. He decided to have a Christmas program and needed Emily to accompany the children on the piano. The children would portray the Christmas story, sing, and recite verses. This would be the first Christmas since the end of the war and his first as pastor of a church. He longed to celebrate the Savior's birth in a spirit of love and peace. The congregation supported his plan with enthusiasm.

At each practice Robert Harris attempted to befriend Emily and call her by her given name. She corrected him each time saying, "It's Miss Mason."

Emily held herself as aloof as possible, but during the practices she caught herself watching the young man as he worked with the children. He had an unusual way with them and she saw they were trying hard to please him. He smiled a great deal and she noticed the patience and gentleness he displayed.

The program would be fairly simple, since they would have such a short time to prepare for it, but she had to admit the production itself would be a meaningful one. The children learned their parts and the parents offered help with the stage and costumes. Robert Harris worked hard, knew what he was doing, and carried the program out according to plan.

The day of the final practice Emily arrived early. She planned to go over the music before the children appeared. As she was playing, Robert Harris came out of his study and approached the piano. "I wish you'd let me call you by your given name. Miss Mason sounds so formal after all these weeks."

"Only my close friends call me by my given name," she answered coolly.

"Can't we be friends, Emily? I'd like that."

"It's Miss Mason, and we hardly know each other."

"We could get to know one another, if you'd talk to me. May I call on you at your home some afternoon?"

Emily ignored his question and continued to play softly. "Excuse me, Reverend Harris. I need to practice so I'll be ready for the children when they come."

❧

Meanwhile, Frederic, who had brought Emily into town that day, was trying hard to make Collette understand his feelings.

Collette was visiting her aunt and uncle's place for the holidays, and Frederic had visited her several times since her arrival. The week before, he had taken her to the farm to join his family for dinner. He wanted her to see the place so dear to his heart. His own enthusiasm for the farm did not persuade her, however. Collette ignored the farm and conversed about Portland and her father's business. She explained the trade opportunities to other parts of the world and described the massive sailing vessels. The whole family noticed her indifference to their way of life.

Today Frederic would face Collette with his decision. Many nights he had slept little as he had wrestled with the problem of whether to accept her father's offer of a job, and he had sought earnestly for God's leading. Today, after leaving Emily at the church, he had headed Nell toward the Jordan home.

I'm ready to give my answer and it will be a definite no. I must be true to God's calling for my life, and true to myself. The job in Portland is not what I'm cut out for. I'll stick with farming.

As he tried to explain his decision to Collette that afternoon, she frowned. "My father offered you a chance to be a gentle-man, with a gentleman's position, and you are turning it down?" she asked bitterly. "I can't believe you would choose farming. It's loathsome to me and I could never, never consider being a farmer's wife!"

"That settles it then," Frederic said quietly. "I could never do anything else."

Collette's voice rose angrily. "You prefer farming to me? How could you?"

"I didn't say that. I only know farming is my life. I can't change. Collette, you don't understand. Farming is in my blood. I like the smell of the animals, planting crops and seeing them spring to life from tiny seeds, the feel of the soil as it sifts through my hands. Nothing compares with it. I wouldn't be happy sitting at a desk in a stuffy office. It just isn't me."

"Then it's goodbye, Frederic. I hope you'll enjoy groveling around in the dirt." Collette burst into tears and ran from the room.

A quiet and thoughtful Frederic was shown to the door by Collette's aunt. The older woman surmised something was amiss, but said nothing.

The strain Frederic had been under left him physically drained. He headed Nell toward the little church to pick up Emily for the ride home. Little flakes of snow cascaded from the heavens. The flakes, like little balls of cotton, clung to the trees, but on the ground in front of him they sparkled like diamonds. A cool, brisk air fanned his cheeks, reviving him. He felt a huge load lifting from his shoulders.

Evidently the job opportunity included an understanding Collette and I would marry. Certainly I never broached the subject. Did she read something into my words or actions? I thought we had a strictly friendly relationship. I never should have visited her in Portland. The opportunity came at a time when I needed to get away, but she obviously mis-understood. My intentions were for friendship and nothing else. But Collette is angry. She made it pretty clear that she wants nothing to do with me. . .no friendship, no nothing. What did she say? Farming was loathsome to her? She can't understand my feel for the soil. . .planting the seeds, nur-turing them, and seeing them spring into a bountiful har-vest.

Frederic knew that no matter how hard the work, the end results of farming were rewarding. God had called him to be a farmer, that he knew. His pa and grandpa already knew how hard the life of a farmer could be, but the challenge of the land excited him. He glanced at the little church as he reigned Nell to a halt. "God," he whispered, "with Your help I'll be the sturdiest and best farmer I know how to be."

eighteen

The Christmas program was enthusiastically received. It set the mood for the spirit of Christmas and parents proudly watched their youngsters as they performed. Most agreed the young Mr. Harris did a fine job and just possibly could be exactly what the little flock needed.

The holidays at the Mason farm were a relaxing time spent with the family. The menfolk chose and cut a large pine from the back property. Tree decorations, handmade and kept from year to year, nestled on the pine boughs. Each year the womenfolk added a few new ones, fashioned out of bits of cloth, lace, and ribbon. Fragrant boughs decorated the mantel, while candles burned brightly in several windows, giving a cheery welcome.

Cassie and Bill joined the family for Christmas dinner. Once again they picked up Aunt Maude who would stay with her brother's family for a spell. She spoke out after dinner, ridiculing Frederic for refusing Mr. Jordan's fine offer.

"Why do you turn your back on a position that means wealth and prestige, Frederic? I understand Miss Jordan returned suddenly to her family in Portland. Was that your doing?"

Frederic pondered her question before answering. "Collette left of her own accord. I told her I was a farmer and would always be a farmer. That didn't set well with her. She's against farming as a way of life. In fact she loathes it. Anyway, Aunt Maudie, everything worked together for good."

To avoid further discussion of the subject, Emily sat down at the piano and played Christmas carols. The family crowded around and sang, one of their favorite pastimes. Even Aunt Maude reluctantly joined in and soon got into the spirit. Their voices blended in harmony as the familiar carols filled the air.

Some time later they ended their singing when they heard Laddie barking on the porch. Loud knocking sounded at the door, and Frederic hurried to open it. Sarah Jane, bundled warmly against the chill, entered quickly with cheeks bright pink from the frosty air.

"Merry Christmas!" she called gaily. "Ma sent some currant jelly and Christmas cakes."

Frederic took her wraps and hurried her in by the warm fire to thaw. The family greeted Sarah warmly, and she expressed her delight at the lovely tree and decorations.

"Don't stop your singing," she pleaded. "It sounded so beautiful."

"You must be frozen," Emily cried. "Did you walk all that way alone?"

"Yes," Sarah replied. "Ma said I could come if Bill and Cassie would bring me back on their way home."

"Of course we will," Bill agreed. "We planned to visit the folks later anyway."

At Sarah's insistence they returned to the piano and she joined in with her lilting soprano voice. Finally, tiring, one by one their voices gave out and they relaxed around the fire.

"Sarah, how about a game of checkers?" Emily asked. "We can go into the kitchen and play."

"Sounds like fun," Sarah agreed, and the two headed for the kitchen table. "Let's say the winner starts the second game."

Grandpa and Pa decided on a game of chess at a small table in the corner, while the others lingered lazily by the fireside. They could hear overtones of Emily and Sarah laughing and talking. Their sudden squeals of triumph echoed as they captured a king or made some other exceptional play.

"Sarah Jane is a pretty child," Aunt Maude said. "How old is she now?"

"She's fifteen, Aunt Maudie. Isn't that right, Bill?" Fred asked.

"Yep, fifteen going on twenty-one," Bill laughed. "She wants people to think she's older than she is."

"No need to grow up so fast," Aunt Maude said. "Time gets away from us and we're old before we know it. I wouldn't mind going back a few years. Don't know why she'd want to hasten the aging process. She's at a splendid age. It does do me good to hear the young people laugh and enjoy themselves."

After a few stimulating games, Emily and Sarah rejoined the others. Sarah sat on a low stool off to one side and gazed into the fire. Frederic noticed the red-gold glints in her hair highlighted by the dancing flames. Her small, oval face and creamy complexion reminded him of a delicate cameo his grandmother used to wear.

"Who won the games, Sarah?" Fred asked.

Sarah turned and looked up at Frederic with her violet-blue eyes. "Emily won two out of three," she said thoughtfully. "I'll have to catch her another time."

"Emily is hard to beat. I know. I grew up with her," Fred said smiling. "How's school going for you? I know you're a good student."

"Miss Ragsdale wants me to go on for more schooling after I graduate. I never was interested, but she says I need to look to the future."

"How do you feel about it?" Frederic asked. "Would you like to be a teacher like Miss Ragsdale?"

"Never!" Sarah said emphatically. "Oh, Miss Ragsdale is nice. . .young even. . .and a good teacher. But I wouldn't want to teach like she does, to a bunch of students. Miss Ragsdale handles them well, but I wouldn't have the patience."

"Maybe some other field, then?" Frederic asked.

"If I did go on for more schooling, I'd be a nurse. I always like taking care of our animals when they need fixin' up. It's a good feeling to ease their pain. Guess it would be even more rewarding to take care of people. . .and know you could do something to help them. More and more women are doing that now, you know."

"That would be a mighty fine calling, Sarah. And I know you'd be good at it, caring the way you do. I think you'll succeed at whatever you take up."

Ma decided it was time for a supper-snack for everyone, and she pulled out the leftovers. Cassie and Emily helped put out sliced turkey, homemade bread, canned pickles, Ma's special fruit cake, the currant jelly and cakes, and various pies. As the group gathered around the table, Ma brought a pitcher of frothy, hot mulled cider, spiced with cinnamon. Mugs were passed down the checkered tablecloth until each person had one. The frothy brew was sweet to the taste and warming to the body.

"How do yer folks like the new preacher, Sarah?" Pa asked as he passed her the plate of turkey.

"They think he's a fine preacher, Mr. Mason," Sarah answered. "Pa usually goes over his message each Sunday during dinner. Says he can't find a thing wrong with his preaching."

"We think he's a good un," Grandpa said. "Leastwise, most of us do."

"I thought he did sech a fine job on the Christmas program," Ma added. "Ya could see he put a lot o' time into it."

"And you had a big part in it yourself, Emily," Sarah said. "Your piano accompaniment was lovely."

"Thanks, but it was the children who made the program so beautiful. They worked very hard," Emily stated.

Emily observed that Sarah, sitting by Frederic, seemed quite grown up. In fact, she was fast becoming a very pretty young lady. Her freckles were fading and her red-gold hair hung loosely curled about her shoulders. Foregoing her usual garb, she wore an attractive soft blue wool dress which highlighted her violet-blue eyes. It seemed Sarah Jane had taken Emily's advice about dressing in a more feminine style. Emily knew, without a doubt, that Sarah felt a great attraction for Frederic. None of the others suspected, she was sure, and least of all Frederic. He joked and talked with Sarah completely unaware of her growing affection for him.

"Sarah, where are you putting all that food?" Frederic teased. "I thought sure a little thing like you would eat like a bird."

"Ho, look at your own plate, would you!" Sarah said quickly. "Do you plan to stuff yourself like Mr. Turkey?"

"Fred, ya hush!" Ma said. "Quit teasin' Sarah Jane. She's not eatin' much at all. And we have plenty."

"Just gettin' her goat up, Ma," Fred laughed.

Frederic felt an easiness talking to Sarah. He had not spoken to her, except briefly at church, since that day back in November when they went horseback riding, but now they talked at some length, discovering they had several things in common. Both appreciated good music, good books, the outdoors, and of course, horses.

Later, when Cassie, Bill, and Sarah left, the family relaxed around the fireplace again. The logs snapped and crackled as the flames shot upward, dancing and glowing brilliantly.

The family discussed this month's convening of the United States Congress. With twenty-seven states having approved it, the Thirteenth Amendment to the Constitution, abolishing slavery, was formally put into effect.

"President Lincoln signed the Emancipation Proclamation back in January, 1863," Frederic noted. "But that meant only the slaves in the rebel states were free, didn't it?"

"That's right," Grandpa declared. "But now they've finally passed this here amendment and all blacks are free. Abe Lincoln, if he were alive, would be mighty pleased."

"They say that the war wasn't about slavery," Frederic ventured, "but I dare say it was the underlying cause."

"War is in man's nature," Pa added thoughtfully. "He'll find a reason. It's allus been that way. There will be wars and rumors o' wars, accordin' to the Bible. I pray to God that there will never be another as bloody and terrible as this one."

One by one the older generation left for bed, leaving Emily and Frederic alone. They watched the fire curl upward for some moments before Emily spoke. "Big brother, are you aware of your ardent admirer?"

"Admirer? What are you talking about?"

"Sarah Jane. She adores you and you can't see it, can you?"

"You always were a tease, Emily. Sarah Jane doesn't give beans about me. She's a youngster. There must be a dozen young men to catch her eye. I'm an old man. . .a crippled one at that. She did tell me once it didn't matter. But hey, she's just fascinated because I've been to war."

"I knew you didn't recognize her feelings. She's not a child anymore. She's grown up quickly over this past year and she converses in a mature manner. You must have noticed that."

"Well, I do enjoy talking to her, and we found we have a lot in common. She has a level head on her shoulders. . .she's not giddy and light-headed like some young women."

"I dare say she understands her emotions, and they are very strong ones."

"Well, if that doesn't beat all." Frederic was stunned. "If

you are right, I'd best be on my guard. I must take care not to encourage her."

"Why not? Sarah is a lovely young lady."

"It takes time to heal, Emily. I can't think about anyone seriously right now."

"You still care for Becky Sue, don't you?"

Frederic gazed into the fire for several moments searching for the right words. "Becky Sue is only a memory that lingers in my mind sometimes. She was my childhood sweetheart. I thought we were in love. We planned a life together for after the war. But time changes things, and life goes on. I'm grateful she and Zack are back together again. I hope they will always be happy." He shook his head. "No, I don't care for Becky Sue anymore, not like I did. But Sarah—I couldn't—" He shook his head again, feeling both bewildered and strangely pleased.

nineteen

Through the long, hard Maine winter the women baked bread; mended, sewed, darned, and knitted clothing, quilted bed covers, and hooked rugs. The menfolk donned heavy woolen caps and shirts, and wore snow packs on their feet as they spent much time in the woods. The harsh winter had unpredictable thaws that sent the maple sap flowing and the farmers scrambling to gather it. They drilled the holes, caught it in tin buckets, and carried it out of the woods by horse-drawn sleds. The men also hunted, fished, and trapped. Cutting and hauling wood to take to the saw mill took up much of the daylight hours. Firewood had to be cut and split continually to keep the cook stove and fireplaces supplied.

Frederic took Aunt Maude home on a cold and crisp winter afternoon. Emily, trunks piled high with her belongings, rode along. She was moving to Aunt Maude's in town where she would begin her college studies at Colby.

Soft, pure white snow touched the evergreens, graced the maples, and covered stone fences. Frederic hitched up the sleigh as the roads were packed and icy from the abundant snowfalls. Nell snorted in the brisk air. Her thick winter coat glistened in the sun as she pulled her passengers safely to their destination.

Frederic unloaded Emily's trunks and many packages. "Looks like you've got everything you own," he teased. He carried them into one of the bedrooms upstairs in the magnificent brick home.

Maude had a cook/housekeeper, Martha, and a neighboring

handyman, Zeke, to help keep her home running smoothly. She had become accustomed to such amenities when her husband had been alive and could continue them now that he was dead for he had left her comfortably well off.

Emily, excited about starting college, bubbled with enthusiasm. Her friend, Louisa Bradford, would start Colby at the same time, and they hoped to share several classes. Louisa lived in Waterville, near the Common, and they expected to spend much leisure time together. "Louisa and I can hardly wait to get started. It'll be such fun."

"It's what you've always wanted, Emily," Frederic said. "I'm glad it's all worked out. I need to say goodbye, though, and get back to the farm. Pa and Gramps will be working in the woods. They need me."

"Go along, Frederic. Thanks for all your help."

"Try and be good and don't get in Aunt Maudie's hair," he teased, giving her a hug.

"I declare, Fred. . .I'm always good. We get along just fine, don't we, Aunt Maude?"

"We do indeed, child, and I'll be appreciating the company. So get along with you, Frederic."

Emily spent the rest of the afternoon settling in. She had brought enough of her personal things to feel right at home. Of course she had spent many other times with Aunt Maude, but that was different. Those were just visits and always ended too soon. This seemed pretty final. Her stay would last until she finished school.

She relaxed herself on the large four poster with its soft quilts and coverlet, and let her eyes take in the loveliness of the room. Twin hurricane oil lamps stood on the polished cherry chest and table. French wallpaper in soft pink roses with matching curtains, an ornate gold framed mirror, and an exquisite English bowl and pitcher on the walnut commode completed the beauty of the room.

When her aunt called her for dinner, she was surprised at how quickly the time had passed. "What fun to be waited on," she murmured. "Dinner is all prepared and ready to be served. I like this kind of life. I think I was born for this."

After dinner Aunt Maude had an unexpected caller. When Emily realized it was Robert Harris, she made an excuse to leave the room, using the pretense of helping Martha with the dishes. Her aunt would have none of it.

"Emily, sit down. Rev. Harris has come to call and I'm sure he would enjoy talking to both of us."

The Rev. Harris was indeed pleased to see Emily for he had not expected to find her there. He made social calls on members of his congregation during the week. The fact that Emily happened to be there was a pleasant and welcome surprise.

After inquiring about Aunt Maude's health, he looked directly at Emily. "Did you have a pleasant Christmas with your family, Miss Mason?"

"Fine, thank you, Rev. Harris," she replied and looked quickly away. When she turned back, she saw him watching her intently. When she had no further conversation, he turned to her aunt.

"Mrs. McClough, how are things with you? Is there any way I can help you? As your pastor, I want to be of service if you need anything."

Maude expressed her thanks for his concern and assured the young pastor that everything was fine. "Did you know that my niece will be staying with me while she attends Colby College? She's the only one of Chase's children with enough wit about her to go on with higher schooling. I wanted Cassie and Frederic to attend but they refused. At least Emily has her priorities in the right place."

Robert Harris smiled. "I'm sure you will be an excellent student," he said glancing at Emily. "What courses do you plan to study, Miss Mason?"

"Fiddlesticks!" Aunt Maude exploded. "Don't be so formal, young man. You must call her Emily. That's her given name."

"Thank you, Mrs. McClough. I would like to very much."

"I plan to be a teacher, Rev. Harris," Emily stated coolly. "I'm not sure what my classes will be as yet. Whatever is necessary for a degree in teaching little children."

"I'm sure you will be a fine teacher one day, Emily. Emily." Softly he said her name again and then hesitated. "It's a nice name."

Their eyes met and held briefly before she glanced away.

twenty

Emily threw herself enthusiastically into her studies. She and Louisa shared most of their classes and they often stayed on at the college to study and do research. She was busy and she rarely got home to the farm.

Aunt Maude enjoyed having her niece with her and appreciated their visits late in the evening before bed. Emily related happenings at school, and Maude, gratified that at least one of her brother's children was taking advantage of higher education, shared her excitement. Although Maude tended to be bossy and Emily high-spirited, they formed a truce early on, hoping to avoid any clash of a serious nature.

Robert Harris called frequently on the Widow McClough, hoping each time for glimpses of Emily. Often he would be there when she arrived home from Colby. She would come bouncing into the room, bubbling over with witty bits of Shakespeare from her literature class, and Robert was eager to discuss it with her.

Emily stubbornly held him at a distance, though, responding coolly but courteously. Still, he persisted and eventually, in spite of herself, she found herself warming toward this kind and humorous young man. She began anticipating his visits and felt disappointed when he missed several days in succession. He told amusing stories, catching her off guard, and she laughed in spite of herself. She found herself looking at him quickly from time to time, catching him looking at her with a soft, wistful expression that warmed her blood.

After one of his visits, he bade her farewell and took her

small hand in his larger one, holding it briefly. Emily felt a tremor of excitement at the warmth of his touch, and color rushed into her cheeks.

"I can see who the reverend is really interested in seeing," Aunt Maude said bluntly after Robert left.

"Oh, Aunt Maudie, of course he comes to see you. I just happen to be here too."

"That young man has a serious look about him, Emily. I don't doubt he has marriage on his mind." Aunt Maude always came straight to the point. "The life of a preacher's wife is a hard one and you don't want that. Mind my words, child. You finish your schooling and become a teacher. Don't get sidetracked!"

"Fiddlesticks, Aunt Maudie. Marriage is the farthest thing from my mind."

Warm thoughts of Robert Harris flashed through Emily's mind, however, more often than she cared to admit. His serious deep green eyes and crooked grin had caught her fancy. His entire face lit up when he smiled, which was often. But marriage—well, of course that was out of the question.

&

Toward the end of February, Aunt Maude came down with a chill. She'd gotten her feet wet, refusing to wear her boots, and now had the croup. She took to her bed and wouldn't eat, coughing laboriously late into the night. The doctor feared it would go into pneumonia, and he limited her visitors to the family and the preacher. Frederic and the family came, but under doctor's orders, stayed only a few minutes.

The "grip," as Maude called it, hung on into March and then she seemed to rally and do better. Emily constantly tried to get soup and liquids into her. Maude, feeling stronger, determined to get up and go downstairs, against the doctor's orders.

"I'm better. I'm better," she insisted. "Let me be!"

Emily could not deter her. Aunt Maude would do as she pleased. But as the doctor feared, she took a turn for the worst. Pneumonia took over and gripped her body with a vengeance. Her once stout, robust figure quickly became frail and emaciated, until she became a whisper of the woman they'd known.

Emily neglected school to nurse her beloved aunt, ministering medicine and encouraging liquids whenever possible. By the end of March, Maude had wasted away and breathed laboriously amid constant coughing and spitting.

One morning after a difficult night, she took Emily's hand and whispered faintly, "Emily, dear child, I want you to have my home and all my fine furniture. I know you will care for the house and all my nice things."

"Hush, Aunt Maudie, hush!" Emily cried, bending close to her aunt. "Don't say such things! You're going to be fine. You're going to get well. . .I know you are!"

After a fit of coughing, Maude continued with difficulty. "No, child. I'm ready to go. I'll see my Maker and my beloved George. He's been waiting for me."

"No, Aunt Maudie, no! Don't say such things. I can't bear to hear you talk like that. You'll be better tomorrow. . .much better."

The faint trembly voice continued amid spasms of coughing. "There's money set aside for your schooling. The rest will be divided between Cassandra and Frederic. The house is for you. Cassie has her home with Bill, and Frederic won't leave the farm. You will take care of my house."

Emily burst into tears and threw her arms around Maude's frail, wasted body.

"Don't cry, child," Maude whispered sternly. "I've already talked to your father about my desires and he'll have it taken care of with my lawyer. Now I'm tired, dear child." She waved

Emily away weakly. "I'm so tired."

Emily stumbled blindly from the room, her eyes brimming with tears, and bumped into Robert Harris in the hallway.

"I'm so sorry," she faltered. "I wasn't watching where I was going."

Robert Harris put his strong hands on her shoulders to steady her. "Emily, what's wrong? Has Maude taken a turn for the worst?"

"Yes, she's very bad." Emily was sobbing openly now, the tears streaming down her cheeks.

Robert released her and pulled out a clean handkerchief. "Let me wipe away your tears," he said. Gently he stroked her face, but the tears kept falling. "Is the doctor here?" he asked. "There may be something else he can do."

"He'll be here later today, but Aunt Maude needs him now," she cried. "She's very tired. She sent me away so she can get some rest."

"I'll go in and pray with her," Robert said. "If she is already asleep, I'll still pray for her. God loves Maude and He cares about her. Will you be all right?"

"Yes," Emily answered wiping away more tears. "I'm going to check with Martha and make sure we have plenty of chicken soup. When Aunt Maude wakes up, she'll need some broth and tea."

Twenty minutes later Robert Harris descended the stairs and entered the kitchen. Emily and Martha were preparing chickens to make a broth so that it would be ready when Maude wakened. Emily looked up from her task. "How's Aunt Maudie? Is she awake?"

"She's sleeping quite peacefully at the moment," Robert said. "I'm sure the rest will be good for her."

"Did you pray? Did you pray and ask God to heal her?"

"Yes, I prayed. I asked God for healing of Maude's body.

Then I committed Maude to His keeping and prayed His will be done."

"But it is His will for Maude to be healed. Why didn't you demand God heal her?"

"Emily, we don't demand God to do anything. He is God . . .He is in control. The Bible tells us to pray 'according to His will.' He knows the end from the beginning, and what is best for all His children."

"I don't care. . .I want Aunt Maudie to live!"

"We all do, if it's His will. The church people are praying. I'll be back tomorrow, Emily, or sooner if you need me."

Emily closed the door as Robert left, then she turned back to the kitchen. "Don't you let her die, God," she cried fiercely. "Don't you dare let her die!"

twenty-one

Maude McClough lingered until mid-April and then passed away in her sleep. The frail body could hold up no longer, and she was tired of fighting for life. She was reconciled to her Maker and ready and willing to go.

Emily became quiet and withdrawn. She believed God had failed her. He had not answered her prayers for healing, and she could not accept Maude's death. She went through long periods of crying, praying, and asking God, "Why?"

The service held in the little church was Robert Harris' first funeral. Emily refused to attend, and so she did not hear the message of comfort and hope.

"We will all miss Maude McClough," Robert Harris told them. "She was a fine Christian woman. When something like this happens, it's hard to understand God's ways. We would rather have our sister here with us still. It's hard to understand how a loving God could take her away from us now, when we had expected to have many more years together." He shook his head. "I can't deny that death hurts. Even Jesus wept when his friend Lazarus died. But we know from God's Word that our sister Maude has gone to a far better place. . .where there is no pain, no sickness, no sorrow. She is at peace, living in heaven with her Lord. And though we are sad now, this story will have a happy ending, for one day we will see her again."

The Rev. Harris went on to quote many portions of Scripture and closed with Psalm 116:15: "Precious in the sight of the Lord is the death of his saints."

They buried Maude in the little cemetery behind the church. She was placed next to her husband George and near her mother and a sister who had died as a child.

Emily would not be consoled. She dropped her college classes and buried herself in her grief. Bitterness toward God gnawed away at her insides, making her miserable. The family tried comforting her but without success; her attitude did not change.

"I can't help how I feel," she said sadly. "Where is God anyway, when we need Him?"

Chase insisted she return home for a spell, but she resisted. The others persuaded him to let her stay in town to work things out alone. She wouldn't be completely alone as Martha, the housekeeper, lived at the house and would remain as long as Emily needed her. Emily's friend, Louisa, lived close by and tried her best to get Emily back to her normal self again.

"Come back to school," she begged. "It will be good for you. Things aren't the same without you. I miss you terribly."

"I can't go back, Louisa. I have to work things out first. I have to understand why God did this and I don't want any pat answers."

Robert Harris called several times but Emily refused to see him. She knew he would criticize her behavior and she couldn't handle that. She needed answers instead.

≈

Spring came and balmy breezes penetrated the air. They reached down and kissed the earth with their soft touch. The birds, perched high in the tree tops, sang their sweet melodies.

Martha hauled mattresses outdoors to sun them and put rugs on the line to beat. She was giving the house "a good turning out" as she called it. This meant an old fashioned spring cleaning from top to bottom. Emily, pale and wan, offered to help, but Martha insisted she rest instead. "Go into the back yard and relax, child. You look so peaked. Do some reading, enjoy the sunshine and the fresh, pure air. It will do wonders for you."

Halfheartedly, Emily obliged. She took her Shakespeare along, hoping to find solace in its pages. She read aloud, "This above all, To thine own self be true, And it must follow as the night the day, Thou canst not then be false to any man."

Beautiful words. But they don't fulfill the need of my heart. From just a little girl I was taught to turn to the Bible for comfort and strength. How can I now, when I am at odds with the Author? He's failed me. Will I ever have faith again? Will I ever have faith to believe He can help in times of need?

Emily glanced around her. Everything was coming alive, and the apple trees and lilacs had burst forth in full bloom. Maude's flower gardens were a veritable show place, for she had taken pride in spending endless hours planting, weeding, transplanting, and nurturing. Some of her favorites included the twin flowers, purple lilacs, daffodils, violets transplanted from the woods, ground phlox, and yellow scotch roses.

Emily eyed the plants, some already blooming and others which would soon be transformed into beautiful flowers. She spoke to the plants in a sad voice, "Your mistress, who loved you, is gone. She won't be coming back to enjoy your beauty." Emily felt tears trickling down her cheeks.

"Emily, may I speak with you?"

Emily glanced up to see Robert Harris standing just outside the gate.

"I thought I heard you back here in the garden," he continued. "I've been trying to see you for weeks."

"I didn't want to talk to you," she mumbled, dabbing her eyes with her handkerchief.

"I'm sorry. Do you want me to go?"

She sighed. "You may stay if you promise not to preach to me."

"I'd never do that, Emily. But can we talk?"

Emily agreed they could talk and Robert tried to keep the conversation as light and cheerful as possible as he told of current happenings with the congregation.

"I've missed you, Emily. Everyone at church misses you."

"Can't anyone else play the piano?" she asked absently.

"Mrs. Meade is filling in for now. But that's not what I meant. Emily, when are you coming back to church?"

"Why doesn't God answer prayer?" she countered. "Can you answer that?"

"I'll try if you won't think I'm preaching."

"Then try."

The young pastor was quiet for a few moments, collecting his thoughts. Then he said soberly, "God is not accountable to us for what He does or does not do, Emily. He doesn't have to reveal 'why.' He owes us no explanations."

"God isn't fair. Why would He take Aunt Maude?"

"When we think God is not fair, what are we measuring His fairness against? Who invented fairness? Wasn't it God Himself?"

"You sound just like Frederic!" Emily exclaimed. "He never blames God for anything!" Emily pressed her lips together, and then she burst out, "I don't care if you think I'm awful, I don't care if I'm committing some awful sin. I just don't understand why God could fail me like this."

Robert's lips curved. "I don't think you're awful, Emily. I don't think I ever could. And you're not committing a sin by questioning God. Why, even Christ on the cross felt forsaken and cried out to God." He touched her face gently, then withdrew his hand. "We can't understand everything about God.

We never will. If we did, He wouldn't be God. Sometimes it's hard to trust blindly—but we know He has promised that nothing will ever separate us from His love. When we really believe that, then all our hurt and anger don't really matter anymore, because then we know that everything that comes our way, both good and bad, can never stop God's love from reaching us."

Emily bit her lip. "I don't know," she said at last. "I feel so angry at Him. If I could really believe that Aunt Maude was still alive in heaven, I wouldn't feel so bad. I want to believe it, I want to believe it more than I ever have in my life. And yet I'm filled with so many doubts."

"Your doubts can't change what's real." He took both her hands and pulled her to her feet. "Walk with me through Maude's garden. God touches each of these blossoms and causes them to spring to life. Our lives are like that too. God touched Maude's life and she sprang into everlasting life with Him." Robert stooped down and plucked a violet that had unfolded into a delicate purple blossom. He held it out to Emily. "It's new life," he said softly, "the resurrection. Once it was dead and now it's alive."

Emily stood deep in thought, gazing at the flower for a long time while she held it cupped gently in both her hands.

twenty-two

Sarah Jane Collins was very perceptive for a young lady going on sixteen. She knew Frederic avoided her whenever possible. Brief encounters at church or in town were all she could hope for, and they were not very satisfying.

She had cared for Frederic since before the war between the North and South. She was eleven and he eighteen when he courted her sister Becky Sue. While he served on the battlefield, her childish fascination grew into a deeper, lasting affection. Becky Sue shared Frederic's war letters with her younger sister, not realizing Sarah's feelings for him. Sarah hung on every word, pretending the letters were meant for her. . .even memorizing portions of them. The family knew nothing about her attachment.

Sarah was distressed when she heard Frederic was wounded severely in battle at Appomattox Court House. *Would he die?* When Becky Sue eloped with Zack, she felt a door being opened to her. Would Frederic notice her now? She was fourteen by this time and experiencing grown-up emotions. Could her dreams become a reality?

She didn't mind that Frederic returned home wounded and crippled. The limp wasn't important when he could have lost the leg. Even that wouldn't have mattered, though. The person remained. . .the same boy. . .young man she cared about. Her feelings never wavered, only became stronger and surer since Frederic had returned home.

Frederic showed, on numerous occasions, that his feelings

for Becky Sue were over. She and Zack had worked out their marriage problems and appeared to be happy, especially now that a child was on the way.

Sarah assumed no one else held Frederic's attention. *Frederic is twenty-two and I'm yet fifteen. The war aged him. . .he feels older than he is. He thinks I'm just a child. I'm not a child! How can I get him to see I'm a woman, with a woman's heart?*

She approached him after church the end of May, detaining him in the church yard. A bright sunny day boasted the sweet scent of purple lilacs and apple blossoms.

"Frederic," she asked, "will you come to my graduation? My mother is having a get-together afterwards at our house. Your whole family is invited, but I especially want you to come."

"Are you old enough to graduate, Sarah Jane?" Frederic teased. "How did you manage that? Aren't you a little young?"

"I skipped a grade some years back," Sarah declared testily. "But I'm old enough! At least my teacher thinks so."

"When is it?" Frederic asked, changing to a more serious tone. "The graduation?"

"It's next Friday afternoon, two o'clock at the school. I would be pleased if you'd attend. It's important to me."

Something in her tone of voice caught at Frederic. She spoke with a pleading quality and her eyes held his without wavering. He found he could not look away from her deep violet-blue eyes.

Suddenly he grinned, reached out, and patted her on the head. "I'll come, little one. I wouldn't miss it for the world."

She smiled and her eyes whispered her thanks. *He still considers me a child, patting me on the head. But at least he's coming! I'll find some way to prove I'm a grown-up and not*

the little freckle-faced kid he remembered when he left for
the war. Mama was married at sixteen and I'll be sixteen in
the fall. That's a good age.

ಇ

Frederic rode his horse and arrived at the school for the graduation exercises the following Friday as promised. His family,
the Collins, and other spectators were already there. The students thronged together in the school yard, waiting until time
to march in. Each grade would march in procession, with the
graduates last.

Frederic's own graduation seemed so long ago to him, and
yet like yesterday in some ways. Since then, though, had come
the war years, the battles, his disability, and the time in the
hospital. Suddenly, he felt very old and questioned why he
had come. His eyes searched the group for Sarah Jane, and
he discovered her standing under a tree, surrounded by several male students.

As soon as she spied him, she called out and waved.
"Frederic! Frederic! I'm so glad you came." She wore a lovely
sea green dress with a large lace collar, clasped at the throat
with a cameo brooch. Her red-gold hair seemed redder than
usual. It was tied with green ribbons and fell in a mass of
curls about her shoulders. Her youthful, creamy complexion
glowed with a tint of color on her cheeks.

Frederic viewed this lovely creature hurrying toward him
and caught his breath. Sarah took his large hand in hers and
pulled him, limping, toward the others.

"Are those young men all your beaus, Sarah Jane? I'm not
surprised you have so many."

"Of course not, silly," she replied laughing. "They're just
youngsters. . .kids in school."

"Youngsters?" Frederic quipped. "Youngsters, like you?"

Sarah faced him squarely, her violet-blue eyes intent upon his. "I'm not a youngster, Frederic. Not any more. Can't you see that I've grown up? Can't you see that I'm a woman?"

Frederic gazed steadily at this grown-up vision of loveliness. He agreed in his heart that she was, indeed, a woman.

twenty-three

Frederic thought about Sarah Jane as he rode over to the Collins' farm for her graduation party. She was a lovely creature and he struggled with his rising emotions. The deep and special feelings he once had for Becky Sue were gone. Only memories remained and they no longer pulled at his heart. He was a prisoner set free, no longer shackled by a lost love. Now that his heart was free, he was ready and able to love again.

"But Sarah is too young for me," he muttered. "I shouldn't be thinking about her like this. She needs someone her own age, one of those young men I saw at the school. There were several who seemed stricken with her."

Frederic tied Torch to a post and joined the group of family and friends gathered in the back yard. He spied Sarah Jane over by the punch bowl, talking to one of the young men he had seen earlier. Sarah smiled and waved. As he turned away, he almost bumped into Becky Sue and Zack.

"Hello, Frederic," Becky Sue said smiling, as she clung to Zack's arm. "I guess you heard about our expected little one."

"That's great news," Fred stated. "I'm very happy for you."

"We'll be a real family now," Zack stated. "It's made a big difference in our lives."

"Frederic," Becky Sue paused. "I want to thank you for what you did. You helped bring Zack and me back together again. We'll be forever grateful." She reached out and lightly took Frederic's hand in an expression of friendship.

"Yes," Zack added as he shook Fred's hand wholeheartedly.

"We appreciated your wise counsel. We took it and we couldn't be happier."

"It was nothing," Fred insisted. "I'm just glad the way things worked out."

"Here you are, Frederic!" Sarah Jane said taking his arm. "Come with me. . .I want you to meet my teacher, Miss Ragsdale. Will you excuse us, Becky Sue?"

"Of course, Sarah. You two run along."

Sarah half-pulled him toward the punch table where an attractive brunette was talking to Mr. Collins.

"Whoa, Sarah, not so fast," Fred cautioned. "Remember this bad leg of mine."

"Oh, fiddle," Sarah laughed, "it's as fit as can be!"

Somewhat out of breath, she cornered Miss Ragsdale. "Miss Ragsdale, I'd like you to meet Frederic Mason. You met the rest of his family earlier."

"Yes, I remember. How do you do, Mr. Mason." Hannah Ragsdale looked at him keenly with dark, wide set eyes. "It's a pleasure to meet you."

"The pleasure is mine, Miss Ragsdale," Frederic said, taking the hand she extended.

"Why don't you two get acquainted," Sarah suggested. "Ma told me I had to mingle with the guests. There are plenty of chairs over there by the oak tree."

"Good idea," Frederic said. "Miss Ragsdale, would you care for some cake and punch?"

"Thank you, I would. Please call me Hannah. And may I call you Frederic?" she asked demurely.

"I wish you would. Frederic. . .or Fred, either one Miss, er Hannah."

Hannah laughed as she settled herself into one of the wooden chairs under the large oak tree. Frederic noticed her fair complexion and delicate hands, which she folded in her lap. When she smiled, her eyes sparkled, and her otherwise plain features transformed magically into something pretty.

"Hannah, I've heard what a good teacher you are," Frederic said. "Do you enjoy teaching?"

"I do very much. As to my being a good teacher, I'm afraid Sarah Jane is prejudiced. She's a very bright girl. I hope she'll go on and get some more education. She has the mind for it."

Frederic wasn't certain how long he and Hannah Ragsdale talked together. When he saw the crowd thinning out, he felt it was time to make his departure. On an impulse, he invited Hannah Ragsdale to the band concert the following week in Waterville.

"How delightful!" she exclaimed. "I would love it!"

After getting her address and setting the time, Frederic bade her farewell. He searched for Sarah to say goodbye, and found her talking to an older couple from the church. She saw him coming and hurried to meet him. "Fred, you're not leaving, are you? We haven't had time to talk to one another."

"I need to get home, Sarah, and help Pa with evening chores. A lot of people have left already."

"I hoped you'd stay on. Did you and Miss Ragsdale get acquainted? She's such a nice person."

"We found we had a lot to talk about," Fred answered. "And you're right, she's a very pleasant person."

Sarah fell into step with Frederic as he headed toward his horse.

"Before I leave," he said, "I have a small gift for you. . .for your graduation. It's in my saddle bag."

"Fred," she cried, "you bought me a present? Really?"

"Really," he said, smiling at her excitement. *She's such a child*, he told himself. *A sweet child, and so pretty, but just a child and. . .* He could feel her close presence as he fumbled in his saddle bag for her gift. She brushed against him and he breathed in the sweet, delicate scent of lilacs. *She's just a child*, he reminded himself sternly, but his pulse was pounding.

"Congratulations, Sarah," he said huskily as he handed her a neatly wrapped package.

"Thank you, Fred." She tore open the wrapping and held up a small volume of poetry.

"It seemed right for you, Sarah. I hope you like it." He had spent a long time deliberating over what to give her. He watched her face, hoping he hadn't made the wrong choice.

She opened the book to the flyleaf page and read aloud: "To Sarah from Frederic, June 1866." Then she clasped the book to her and looked up at him. Her eyes were moist and wistful. "I love poetry," she said softly. "It's something I've always wanted. I'll cherish this book, Fred."

Frederic gazed at her sweet, upturned face and felt a sudden desire to take her in his arms and hold her close. Instead, he took a deep breath and said, "I'm glad you care about it, Sarah. I like poetry, too."

For a long moment, their gazes locked, as though time had frozen around them. *She's just a child, just a child, just a child*, Fred was repeating over and over inside his head, but the words were meaningless. He wanted to touch her so badly that his muscles ached from holding them still.

He swallowed hard and swung himself into the saddle. "I'll be seeing you, Sarah," he managed to say, and then he trotted Torch down the drive. When he looked back, she waved. She was still standing in the same spot. . .watching him go.

"Why did I ask Hannah Ragsdale to the band concert?" he mumbled. "She's a sweet and interesting person, and we'll have a good time. But I'm afraid Sarah Jane will be on my mind most of the time. There's something unique about her. She's special. I can't pinpoint it actually, but I get sort of light-headed when she's around. Just thinking about her makes me feel happy inside. Only then I remember I shouldn't be feeling that way. Not when I'm so much older than she is."

He nudged Torch into a gallop and felt the early summer breeze caress his face. "Yep, Torch, that young lady has my heartstrings all entangled. I just wish she wasn't so young!"

twenty-four

Robert Harris visited Emily several times after their talk in the garden. She was more receptive with each call as he pointed out God's love and promises from the Scriptures. Emily asked if she had been a disobedient Christian. . .angry with God and asking why Aunt Maudie had died.

Robert smiled and shook his head. "Everyone has doubts sometimes. Even the authors of some of the Old Testament books asked God why sometimes. I think maybe our faith grows the most during those times when we're filled with doubts. We'll never know all the answers," Robert told her. "We just need to trust God, and claim His promises from His Word. You will see your Aunt Maude again some day."

Robert's words were a soothing balm to her heart. After his visit, Emily fell on her knees and poured out her heart to God. "Forgive me for not trusting You in every situation. I have been so miserable because I've been out of fellowship with You, and other Christians. Please, God, fill me with the mind of Christ."

Emily felt God's presence wash over her. His peace and comfort drew her close. She no longer felt at odds with her Maker. "I'll go back to the farm," she cried. "The folks have put up with my bitter attitude and pouting long enough! Oh, it will be so good to be with the family again! I'll spend the summer at home!"

Immediately she made preparations to return and left Martha in full charge of the house in town.

The family greeted her with open arms. Emily felt like a

prodigal returning after a life away from God and the comforts of family. They had been waiting for her to come out of her depression and return home.

"I'm still sad over Aunt Maudie's death, the same as all of you," she told them. "But I'm not asking God why anymore. I don't need to know why things happen. I accept with faith what He sends. . .what He gives and what He takes."

Chase and Mary Jane rejoiced at the change in their daughter. She had accepted Maude's death and matured from the experience. Cassie and Bill joined the family for supper that evening, looking as happy and as much in love as ever.

"We have some wonderful news, Emily," Cassie confided, smiling. "I'm going to have a baby."

Emily shrieked with delight and hugged her sister. "How wonderful! I'm so happy for you both. When. . .?"

"Around Christmas or there-abouts." Cassie replied.

"He will be our special Christmas gift," Bill stated proudly. "This will be the best Christmas ever!"

"Bill. . ." Cassie said sweetly. "It might be a girl."

"Either one. . .it will still be our special Christmas gift," he said kissing her lightly on the cheek.

That evening the talk centered around the new baby. The family had known about it earlier, but they shared in the excitement of the moment.

"So everyone knew but me? Why didn't I hear this good news earlier?" Emily demanded.

"Cassie thought it best ta wait," Ma offered. "We all agreed ya had enough on yer mind."

"We wanted you to work through your unhappiness, first," Cassie murmured. "We knew you would, in time."

"I'm afraid I wasted a lot of time feeling sorry for myself," Emily said. "I learned a lesson through this. God is always there waiting for us to come to Him."

"Just think, I'll be an uncle," Frederic said lightheartedly. "Uncle Fred, the farmer. It sounds good."

"Do you have any names picked out?" Emily asked. "I suppose it will be Bill Junior if it's a boy."

"No Juniors," Bill said emphatically. "I like Ethan or Jeremiah, but we've not settled on anything."

"I think we'll name a little girl Rebeccah," Cassie said softly, "after Grandma."

Grandpa smiled broadly. "Thet would be a fine name, Cassie. Yer grandma would a' been proud."

"Grandpa made the cradle and Ma and I are working on the layette," Cassie said. "Why don't you come over tomorrow and see the nursery, Emily? You can help me with some sewing."

"Oh, I'd like that," Emily agreed.

"We need Emily in the field, don't we Pa? With it being seed planting time and all. You plan to help us at five tomorrow morning, don't you, Emily?" Frederic teased.

Emily smiled. "Yep, Frederic. After I show you, Pa, and Gramps what to do in the fields, I'll hustle over to Cassie's and sew!"

"Now, dear. . .yer brother was jest foolin'," her mother stated soberly. "The men folk do the farmin'. We got woman's work ta do."

"Just teasin', little sister," Fred agreed. "By the way, Robert Harris asked about you at church."

"Is that young man interested in ya, Emily?" Grandpa asked.

All eyes turned toward Emily and she felt color rising in her cheeks. "We are good friends, Grandpa. Robert Harris called on me last week and we talked. He helped me get my thoughts straightened out and work through my bitterness. He was very kind."

"Does he have marriage on his mind?" Grandpa persisted.

"Seems like he's up in the clouds lately."

"He's not discussed anything like that," Emily said embarrassed. *Why do I blush so easily?* "I'm sure marriage is not on his mind."

The following day Emily spent with her sister at the cabin. They talked, sewed, and laughed like old times and their good time had a therapeutic effect on Emily. "You are so blessed, Cassie. A fine husband and now a baby coming. I'm very happy for you."

"You'll find happiness some day, Emily, when you marry a fine young man. . .like Robert Harris, for instance. I know you are attracted to him."

"He wouldn't want to marry me, Cassie. I wouldn't make a good preacher's wife."

"And why not?" Cassie demanded.

"Look at all the doubts I had about God when Aunt Maudie died. I was bitter. . .only thinking about myself and my loss. A problem comes along and I waver. I'm such a weak Christian. Robert needs someone stronger in her faith."

"Someone like Louisa?"

"Is Robert. . .is he seeing Louisa?"

"They've been together some. But I think his mind is really on you. He's cared for you from the first."

"I've been such a ninny, the way I've treated him. But I want an education. I don't want to get married."

"Are you sure, Emily? Make sure you sort out your feelings. Don't let something you really want pass you by."

"If he cares for Louisa, it's too late anyhow," Emily said sadly. "She's my best friend. I wouldn't want to hurt her."

"What would hurt most? Losing Robert? Ask yourself."

Cassie had touched on a tender subject and Emily couldn't sew any longer. Tears brimmed her eyes and overflowed, till she could no longer see the stitches. She stuck herself with the needle twice. Thoughts raced wildly through her mind.

Does Robert love me? Does he want to marry me? What about school? I've given him no encouragement at all. His eyes spoke to mine many times, and his crooked, endearing smile seemed for me alone. I've probably ruined any feelings he might have had for me by my selfish and bitter attitude toward God. "Cassie," she cried, "why have I been so stupid? I'm in love with Robert Harris!"

Cassie gathered her weeping sister into her arms. The proud Emily had taken the first step. She'd admitted her feelings for Robert and now a healing process could take place.

twenty-five

Later that week, Emily rode into town with Frederic and planned to visit Louisa while he took some pine boards to the mill. He dropped her at the Common and she walked first to Maude's brick home to check briefly with Martha and make certain things were running smoothly. From there, she went directly to the Meade home, secretly hoping to see Robert. Mrs. Meade welcomed her graciously and seemed genuinely pleased to see her.

"We've all missed you at church these weeks, dear," Mrs. Meade said kindly.

"Thank you, Mrs. Meade. I'm doing well now."

"Does this mean you'll be back playing the piano on Sunday?"

"Yes, I'm ready to take over again if you want me to."

"Oh, I certainly do," Mrs. Meade said quickly. "I'm not the player I used to be. I'll welcome you taking it on."

Emily glanced around the room. "Is Pastor Harris here or at the church?"

"Neither, dear, I'm sorry. He's away for the day. Shall I tell him you called?"

"No, thank you," Emily hastened to say. "I just wondered whether he was here. Nothing important."

Emily tried her best to sound nonchalant, but knew Mrs. Meade had seen her disappointment. She made an excuse, said goodbye, and headed toward her friend Louisa's home on Water Street. Lost in her thoughts, Emily walked swiftly along the path, oblivious to the beauty of the day around her. She reprimanded herself for asking about Robert. *What will Mrs. Meade think of me? But then it was a simple question. I was merely curious. Oh, I do hope she understands.*

Emily reached the Bradford home, knocked lightly, and Mrs. Bradford answered the door. "Emily, it's been a while since we've seen you. How nice of you to call. Louisa will be so pleased."

She ushered Emily into the parlor where Louisa was conversing with Robert Harris. Startled at seeing them together, Emily's face turned crimson and she mumbled, "Oh, I'm so sorry to interrupt. I really can't stay."

Louisa jumped up from the divan and grabbed Emily's hand. "You silly goose. . .you aren't interrupting anything. I'm so happy to see you. Come and sit down."

"Yes, Emily," Robert said smiling at her with his crooked grin. "Please stay and visit with us. Louisa and I have been having an interesting conversation."

"Perhaps it's of a private nature," Emily suggested stiffly, as she sat across from them.

Louisa and Robert exchanged mysterious glances. "We are done with that conversation anyway," Louisa said, changing the subject. "Is it nice being home on the farm for a while? Martha said you plan to spend the summer with your family. That will be good for you, Emily. Will you start classes again in the fall? Frankly, I'm glad they are over."

"I'm not sure," Emily faltered. "I've not decided what I'll do as yet."

"Martha says your Aunt Maude left you her house. How generous of her. I suppose you plan to keep it. It's such a lovely old home and furnished so beautifully," Louisa added.

Robert seemed unusually quiet and even a little aloof, Emily thought. He said nothing, but watched her carefully.

"I do love Aunt Maudie's home," Emily said. "The furniture, the garden. . .everything is so beautiful. She was a dear to leave it to me. She knew I loved it and would take care of it."

Robert's lips were set in a firm, unsmiling line. Emily cast quick glances at his face, wondering what his expression meant. She had never seen him look so serious before. Was he resenting her presence there? Had she interrupted an intimate moment between him and Louisa? Emily shifted uncomfortably in her chair. An awkward silence had fallen over all three of them, and Emily was searching for an excuse to take her leave.

Before she could say anything, though, Robert finally spoke. "Will you be coming back to church Sunday, Emily?" His eyes were strangely intent on her face.

"Oh, yes. I've told Mrs. Meade that I'll play the piano again. Thank you, Robert, for helping me get my thoughts together recently. I've overcome my bitterness toward God, I'm happy to say. I was being very childish."

"Not at all," Robert said sincerely, and for a moment his face softened. "You suffered a great loss. Those things take time." He pulled his eyes away from her face, and appeared to be intent upon studying the book titles on the shelf beside him.

Mrs. Bradford came bustling into the room with tea, cookies, and small cakes. As they ate, the conversation turned to lighter things, and they all seemed to relax a little. Still, Emily sensed that Robert was avoiding looking at her, as though something about her displeased him. Had she done something to offend him? He had been so kind about her doubts and anger after Aunt Maude died, but perhaps he disapproved of her now. Perhaps he imagined she would be a bad influence on Louisa.

Emily studied her friend's face, trying to read her expression. She thought Louisa looked unusually pleased with herself, as though she knew some happy secret. Emily's heart sank a little lower. What else could Louisa have been discussing with Robert to make her look like that except love? Louisa and Robert must be in love with each other, and Robert must have just confessed his feelings to her. No wonder Louisa looked so pleased; no wonder Robert was so resentful of Emily interrupting them.

Emily was eager to leave. When Frederic finally arrived for her, she heaved a sigh of relief. She smiled her goodbyes, but underneath she was hurting.

"I'll see you soon," Louisa promised. "We have so much we need to talk about." She smiled, her face secretive again, and glanced quickly at Robert.

Emily returned her smile, but she knew her lips were stiff. She could not force herself to look at Robert. Instead, she mumbled, "I'll see you in church Sunday," while looking down at the gloves she was pulling on her fingers.

"It will be a pleasure to have you once more at the piano, Emily," he answered, but his voice was cold and distant.

Emily hurried out the door before they could see the tears that had risen in her eyes at the ice in Robert's voice. She averted her eyes so that she could avoid looking at either of them, and mumbled her goodbyes over her shoulder.

My best friend and Robert! They certainly are well-suited to each other. Louisa, with her golden hair and pale coloring, is very attractive. How could Robert help but notice how delicate and feminine she is? I must seem drab in comparison. Why didn't I see this coming? Cassie prepared me somewhat, but that doesn't make it any easier. I guess they

*were talking of very private, intimate things when I arrived
. . .perhaps even marriage. My timing couldn't have been
worse. Well, at least now I know the truth. I won't be wast-
ing anymore time thinking about Robert.*

Emily greeted Frederic soberly, then climbed into the wagon
with a heavy heart.

twenty-six

The ride home seemed unusually long. Frederic was very quiet and Emily appreciated the silence. When she finally took a good look at him, she noticed his clothes were disarrayed, his hair rumpled, and he had a small cut on the side of his right cheek.

"What happened to you, Fred?" she cried, reaching out to gently touch his face.

"I had a run-in with someone down at the mill. There I was, minding my own business, but he seemed to want to pick a fight. It was really nothing."

"Why, Frederic? Who was it? Anyone you know?"

"Actually, it's a coincidence because I have met him before. Briefly, while I was at Petersburg during the war. He was assigned to my company for a short time. I remember he was a hot-head. He didn't like me and tried every way he could to show it. . .called me bad names because I said I hated slavery. I pointed out that God created us all equal and no human being should be in bondage to another. He didn't care beans about the black man's plight. He fought simply because there was a war. He seemed to enjoy fighting. The fact that I didn't gamble, curse, or drink with the men bothered him. He called me a sissy, and other names I won't mention. Since I was a captain and he an enlisted man, there were times he had to be disciplined. That galled him and made matters worse."

"Did you try to befriend him, back then?"

"I did, Emily. . .even went out of my way. But he would

have none of it. He hated me and we had several confrontations because of it."

"I wonder what he's doing in Waterville," Emily mused.

"Well, that's it," Frederic said. "I recognized him right away and tried to be friendly. . .forget the past. So I greeted him and asked him why he was in town. He swore and said it was none of my business. Then he shoved me against the boards on the wagon. I shoved back and it turned into quite a scuffle. Zack Turner and his dad pulled us apart, and he left. They don't know anything about the man. . .said he was just hanging around the mill today killing time."

"We don't need his kind around here," Emily said emphatically. "I hope he's just passing through."

❧

They arrived home in time for supper, and their mother had a hot meal waiting. Cassie and Bill were there also. Frederic explained his disheveled appearance and the cut on his cheek, giving them a brief description of what happened.

After supper and a short devotional time, their father said seriously, "I have an important letter to read to you, one that will affect each of you children. That's one reason we asked Cassie and Bill to be here. It's from Maude's lawyer, Josiah Williams, who was a close friend of Uncle George.

"Dated June, 1866. 'Dear Mr. Mason,'" read their father, "'This letter is in regard to the estate of your sister, Maude McClough. I must inform you that George McClough had a son to his first wife, and since Maude's death, he is the legal heir. His whereabouts were difficult to obtain and unknown to me until recently. I have finally located him and he is in town at the present time.'"

"Uncle George was married before he married Aunt Maude?" Frederic asked. "We never knew that."

"Your mother, Grandpa, and I all knew it, and of course

Maude. We knew that George had made a mistake when he was younger, married a girl who left him and ran off with another man. She divorced him, didn't want anything more to do with George. But there was never anything said about a son."

"Maybe he's an imposter," Emily suggested. "Maybe he's someone claiming to be a son so he can get the money and the house."

"Let me finish the letter," Chase said gravely. "'My friend, George McClough, supported this son, through me, for the first eighteen years of his life. His mother was one of low morals but received the money eagerly for the boy's care. However, she refused to let George see or write his son during all those years. The mother passed away two years ago, shortly before George's death. George left instructions that, upon his death, everything go to Maude. But upon Maude's death he directed that everything go to his son and heir, Peter McClough, of Boston. I shall call upon you, along with Peter, on Friday next at 2 p.m. Sincerely, Josiah Williams, Attorney.'"

"That's tomorrow!" Frederic exclaimed. "What a jolt!"

"It's a shock all right," his father agreed, "a real surprise. This means there is no money for you, Frederic or Cassie, no home for Emily, and no money for schooling."

Emily started to cry softly.

"Don't cry, little sister. It's not important, not really," Frederic soothed, placing a comforting arm about her shoulders.

"It's not the house or the money," Emily sobbed. "I never expected them anyway. It's just that an intruder, someone we don't even know, will have the house and all Aunt Maudie's lovely things."

"Well, I hope he's a decent sort of fellow," Frederic said.

"If he's anything like Uncle George, he will be."

Cassie agreed the money didn't matter. She and Bill were too happy to let anything spoil their joy.

"Remember, children," their father cautioned. "Peter McClough has been brought up without a father and by a woman of questionable morals. We don't know what kind of a person he will be. We'll see fer ourselves tomorrow."

"For his sake we must try to be gracious about it," their mother added. "He hasn't been blessed with a lovin' family as ya children have. Cassie, you and Bill best join us tamorra and meet Peter McClough."

"Let's see," Gramps stated, "Maude an' George were married twenty years afore George died two years ago. This young feller must be 'round twenty-five years old. George McClough came here from Boston twenty-four years ago, in April, and set up his medical practice in Waterville. He won yer Aunt Maudie's heart in a hurry. Yep, George was a fine man. We all liked him, and especially yer grandma. George's son Peter has no family now." He paused thoughtfully and added. "Maybe, jest maybe, we can be his family."

twenty-seven

Josiah Williams arrived with his companion promptly at two p.m. the following day, and Mr. Mason ushered them into the parlor where the family had gathered. Mr. Williams was a short, portly man, and his vest stretched tightly across his mid-section. His head was bald except for two patches of grey fringe along both sides. Deep set dark eyes peered from behind spectacles perched carefully on his rather prominent nose. He made a stark contrast to the tall, muscular young man beside him.

Frederic was startled to see that Mr. Williams' companion was Peter Graham, the young man he had found troublesome in the army and again yesterday at the mill. *How could Peter Graham be Peter McClough?* he wondered.

Mr. Williams shook hands with Frederic and his grandfather, then bowed politely to the ladies. "This is Peter McClough, George's son," he stated in introduction. Peter McClough merely grunted, shifting from one foot to the other and eyeing them suspiciously. Peter was well-dressed, just under six feet tall, with a muscular build and dark hair and eyes. He would be considered handsome except for a hardness around his eyes and his firmly set mouth. Peter looked closely at Frederic and said gruffly, "Eh, Mason. . .it's you!"

"Do you know one another?" Josiah Williams asked. "How can that be?"

"Yes, sir," Frederic answered. "We served together for a short time in the war."

"Then you knew him as Peter Graham," Mr. Williams

continued matter-of-factly. "Peter carried his mother's maiden name all those years and I had a difficult time locating him after Maude's death. He's George's son and officially Peter McClough now." Mr. Williams continued to explain George McClough's wishes that were to be carried out upon the event of Maude's death. "He directed everything go to Peter, his son and heir."

"We understand," Chase said. "I've read yer letter ta the family."

"Just want you to get it straight," Peter interrupted hoarsely. "The house. . .the money. . .it's all mine. I'll not share it with any of you."

Josiah Williams spoke up quickly. "Mr. Mason, I have a paper for you to sign. It relinquishes any claims you might have against your sister's estate. I'll need each of the family members' signatures to validate it."

"Of course," Chase agreed. "We have no problem with it. Our daughter Emily had been livin' there with Maude. Maude wanted her ta have the house. Emily will need time ta move her things back home."

"That should be handled as quickly as possible," Josiah Williams suggested. "Peter plans to move into the house as soon as it's vacant and make Waterville his home. He has no family or ties in Boston any more."

After signing the agreement, Mrs. Mason hurried to the kitchen and returned with molasses doughnuts and glasses of cool cider from the spring house.

"Won't ya share in some refreshments?" she asked.

The two visitors eagerly agreed to partake before they started the journey back to town. "This is very kind of you, Mrs. Mason," Josiah Williams murmured. "Very kind indeed, under the circumstances."

"Well, we appreciate meetin' George's son," Grandpa said.

The others nodded their agreement. "We thought a lot o' George. He was a kind and thoughtful man, one o' the best. But we never knew he had a son."

Josiah Williams stood up, consulted the gold watch he pulled from his vest pocket, and prepared to leave. "Folks, thank you for your kindness and cooperation in this legal matter. I have another commitment this afternoon, so Peter and I best be on our way."

"Peter, why don't ya stay ta supper with us tonight?" Mrs. Mason asked. "Frederic can take ya ta town afterwards. Where are ya stayin'?"

"I'm at the Elmwood Hotel temporarily until I move into the house. But I'll pass on the meal," he muttered gruffly.

"Ya'd be welcome," Mr. Mason added. "We'd all like a chance ta get ta know ya."

"Why?" Peter asked quickly. "Why? I won't change my mind, if that's what you think. The money and the house are mine and I intend to have it all."

Mr. Mason put an arm lightly about Peter's shoulders. "We are only interested in ya, Peter, not yer house or yer money. We'd all like ya ta stay, but the decision is up to ya."

Peter shuffled his feet awkwardly, hesitating. *What is with these people anyway? I'm out for all I can get and never mind about them. Why would they want to be nice to me? I'm a stranger to them all except Frederic. And I always hated Frederic and his goody-goody ways. Strange, Frederic hasn't said one word against me.* Peter touched the bruise over his left eye, put there yesterday at the mill by Frederic. He glanced at Frederic's cut cheek. The cut was scabbed over, but there nonetheless. *And Frederic is smiling at me. They all are.*

"I have to leave, McClough. Make up your mind whether you are coming with me," Josiah Williams said.

"Please stay," Mrs. Mason said warmly. "George's son will allus be welcome in our home."

Peter's mouth relaxed from its hard, firm line. He looked at first one and then the other. No one had spoken so kindly to him before. He was a rough character and had been treated as one. This was all new to him. He had to find out if these people were genuine. "I'll stay," he said and managed a slight grin. "It will be a treat to have some home cookin'."

Grandpa and Chase took Peter on a tour of the farm while Frederic tended to the chores. Cassie and Bill headed home, and Emily helped her mother prepare the meal, a delicious boiled ham dinner. Peter ate with a vigorous appetite. Gradually, he began talking about his childhood. "I shifted for myself growing up. Ma wasn't home most of the time. I never did know where she went. She didn't tell me anything about my pa. Just that he was no good. Guess he left her when I was a baby. When I asked about him, she told me he was dead.

"I got out. . .went into the army as soon as they'd take me. It gave me a paycheck. I sent most of it to my ma until she died."

"Yer pa was a fine man. . .a doctor," Chase said. "Ya know, accordin' ta Mr. Williams, he sent money ta yer ma fer yer upbringin'. George was like that. . .took care o' his obligations."

"My ma must have drank up all the money. . .she and her men friends. Oh, she had plenty of them. She never had money left for things we needed, like food and clothes," Peter said bitterly. "I'm afraid I don't have any good memories. I was in Ma's way when I was a kid. I cramped her style. I couldn't wait to get away."

Peter chewed his food thoughtfully, as he reached for another chunk of Mrs. Mason's thick-cut, homemade bread. Methodically, he spread butter and blackberry preserves over its surface. "You say my pa was a good man. . .a doctor in Waterville?"

"His life was dedicated ta the medical profession," Chase replied. "Many a night he didn't get a scrap o' sleep, out carin' fer his patients."

"Yep," Grandpa agreed. "Healin' people and bringin' comfort from pain came first ta George McClough. He was the kind a' man ya can be proud of, Peter."

Peter glanced at the Mason family seated around the dinner table. Their faces expressed an invitation to warmth and friendship. "My old man doesn't sound anything like what my ma described. She couldn't say enough bad things about him. I always figured he was a good-for-nothing slob." He looked down at his plate and added pensively, "I wish I could have known him. I wish I could have known my pa."

twenty-eight

A thoughtful Frederic hitched up the buggy to take Peter back to town. He was grateful Emily decided to ride along. Now he wouldn't have to worry about a lack of conversation. She could handle that, and Peter would be more apt to mind his manners with a lady along.

As they started down the drive, Emily began telling Peter about her aunt's house. "Martha is an excellent housekeeper and cook, if you decide to retain her," she offered. "She's been with Aunt Maude and Uncle George for years. You couldn't find a better one."

"She won't want to stay on with me," Peter said gruffly. "I'm a complete stranger to her. I don't want her living in my house anyway. I can manage alone. I always have."

"You probably won't need Zeke either," Emily continued. "He's a neighbor who has helped Aunt Maude since Uncle George's death...keeping up the place. She paid him of course. I planned to retain them both when I owned the house. But then...things are different now."

"I guess you wish I didn't exist," Peter said cynically. "Now you don't have the house or the money. But they are rightfully mine...you know that!"

"Of course," Emily agreed, smiling. "The house is lovely, you'll see, and the furniture mostly imported. I do love the place, but mainly because I loved the people who lived there ...Aunt Maudie and Uncle George." Tears welled up in her eyes. "But, Peter, I never expected to have the house, not in my wildest dreams, so it's no loss to me. I just hope," she hesitated, then added softly, "I just hope you will care for it and appreciate it. Aunt Maude and Uncle George would want you to."

Peter looked away and didn't respond. They rode for some time in silence, with only the sounds of the horses' hooves clip-clopping on the hard clay roadway.

Frederic finally spoke. "Will you be looking for work in Waterville, Peter?"

"I might," he replied. "I'd like to work at the mill. I've always liked the smell of cut wood. Do you know if they need anyone?"

"No, I don't," Frederic answered. "But my friend, Zack Turner, works there. His pa runs the mill and I'll put in a good word for you."

"You'd do that. . .after the way I've treated you?" Peter asked in amazement.

"Why not?" Frederic asked. "You look like a hard worker, and I know how strong you are." Frederic touched the scab on his right cheek and grinned. "I know firsthand."

Peter McClough sat quietly for some time, as if trying to decide what to say. Finally, he spoke and his voice had lost some of its gruffness. "I'm sorry about how rough I've been, cursing and knocking you around. But hey, you carry a hefty punch yourself." They laughed together and a barrier between them seemed to break.

Emily picked up the conversation once again and chattered about the points of interest in Waterville. In a short time, Frederic stopped the carriage in front of the Elmwood Hotel.

"I'll move my things tomorrow," Emily said as Peter climbed down. "Shall I tell Martha she is no longer needed? And Zeke also? Martha has a sister living nearby that she can move in with."

"I'd appreciate it," Peter replied. "I'd like to go it alone, at least for a while."

"Would you join us for Sunday services?" Frederic asked. "We attend the little community Bible Church here in town. It's the church your pa attended."

"Naw. . .I'm not into church," Peter mumbled quickly. With a wave of the hand, he turned and walked briskly toward the hotel.

They watched as the lonely figure disappeared from sight. With a sigh, Frederic snapped the reins and headed Nell toward home. A soft summer breeze had come up and Emily pushed back straying wisps of hair. "I know he's treated you shabbily, Frederic, but I can't help feeling sorry for Peter."

"Well, he has a fine home now and is financially stable. I'd say he's pretty well set."

"Peter has no family. . .he's really quite alone in this world. It must be a dreadful feeling."

"He's got our family, Emily, if he wants us. We tried to make him welcome. I have no qualms about being his friend."

"When I spent those weeks in town after Aunt Maudie's death, it was unbearable. I was so lonesome. I missed the family, but my pride and anger kept me away. At least I knew I had a family. . .a family that loved me and cared about me."

"Yep, it has to be painful for Peter. He never knew his pa. I'm sure Uncle George loved him, but was unable to see him and express his love. And it's hard to imagine someone like his ma. . .not caring a hoot about him. We have much to be thankful for, Emily. God has blessed us with a loving family."

"Fred, you've been courting Hannah Ragsdale some, haven't you? Do you enjoy her company?"

"Very much. She's a fine person and I admire her. We get along well together."

"I've seen Sarah Jane accompanied by a young man in her

graduating class a few times. He's very handsome and attentive. I wonder if she's interested in him romantically."

Frederic shrugged. "She should be seeing someone her own age. She's so. . .so young."

❧

The following day, Frederic hitched up the wagon for the return trip to Waterville. He and Emily talked at length about their half cousin Peter and the turn of events during the past few days.

Frederic helped Emily load her trunks and other personal belongings on the wagon. Martha and Zeke were told about the new owner and the unusual circumstances of his birth. They were surprised at the news, but neither seemed disturbed.

Emily talked to Martha aside. "I'm so sorry you will be relieved of your position here. You've been with Aunt Maudie for so many years."

"Don't you fret none, child," Martha insisted. "That's just it, I've been working here for a long time. Why, I wouldn't leave Maude as long as she needed me. Then when she passed on, you needed me. Fact is, I'm ready for a change. My sister's been wanting me to live with her for a long time. She's alone too, you know. So it will be good for both of us. I've put some money aside, and we can do some things together. Don't you fret one bit. Everything will be just fine."

Emily hugged Martha and said her farewells. She lingered a time in the garden, noting the brilliant blossoms that seemed to beckon her. *What will become of you?* She took a deep breath and let the delicious fragrance fill her nostrils. "Farewell, sweet blossoms," she whispered, then hurried to the front gate where Frederic was waiting in the wagon.

"Could we stop by Louisa's for a few minutes?" she asked, looking up at him. "I need to talk to her. . .I want to tell her what's happened."

"Yep, I'll drop you off, Emily. I want to go by the mill and talk to Mr. Turner about giving Peter a job."

"I'll walk to Louisa's, Fred. It's such a lovely day. You can pick me up when you're finished."

Emily made her way through town to Louisa's home and was relieved to find her friend alone this time. "I thought I might be interrupting you and Robert Harris again," she said cautiously. "You two were having such a serious and private conversation the other day."

"Nonsense!" Louisa protested. "It was nothing serious."

"Are you quite sure, Louisa? Why were you so mysterious?"

"We didn't mean to be. . .we were just having one of our quiet talks."

"Louisa, are you and Robert in love?" Emily demanded boldly. "I have to know. Is that why he was here?"

"Oh, you silly goose!" Louisa laughed. "You must know that Robert is in love with you. That's what we were talking about. . .you!"

"Me!" Emily's face turned crimson. "What about me?"

"Oh, just how he's been in love with you since the first day he saw you. . .when you fell on the ice and he helped you up!"

"That's ridiculous!" Emily exploded. "People don't fall in love that quickly."

"Not you, perhaps. But Robert claims he did, and I believe him."

"Why was he telling you all this? Why doesn't he tell me?"

"He confided in me since I'm your best friend. Robert is in love with you. . .but says he can't ask you to marry him."

Emily's face paled. "Why not? Oh, I don't blame him really. I've had so many problems accepting Aunt Maudie's death. I neglected church. . .I became bitter. . .I even cried out against God." Emily burst into tears and Louisa gathered her into her arms.

"Dear Emily, that's not the reason," Louisa soothed. "Robert knows you had a difficult time, but you have made your peace with God. He understands."

"Then why, Louisa? Why can't he ask me to marry him?"

"Do you love him, Emily? You must, dear friend. I can tell by your tears."

"I do, Louisa, I do! I think I've loved him for a long time, but wouldn't admit it. I'm so headstrong. . .I wouldn't listen to my heart."

"Robert says he can't ask you to marry him because he has nothing to offer you. You have your aunt's beautiful home, a large amount of money, and all that fine imported furniture. He feels as though he would be marrying you for your inheritance. He's too proud. . .he couldn't bear that."

"Is that all?" Emily asked excitedly, smiling through her tears. She jumped up and whirled around the room. "Oh, he must know the truth, Louisa! It's all too wonderful what has happened. The house, the money, I don't have them after all!"

"What are you saying?" Louisa asked.

Emily sat down, caught her breath, and proceeded to tell her friend all that had transpired during the past few days. "I'm a pauper," she laughed, jumping up again and whirling Louisa crazily about the room. "I can't go back to college. I don't have a house. . .or money. . .or fine furniture. But Louisa, I don't even care!"

twenty-nine

Emily's words regarding Sarah Jane having a beau bothered Frederic. He had decided she was too young for him and had tried his best to keep her out of his mind. But the idea of her enjoying some young man's company filled his thoughts day and night.

"Yer mind isn't on yer work, Fred," Pa said one day while they sat at lunch. "Have ya got a problem? Want ta talk about it?"

"No problem, Pa," Fred said hastily. "Nothing I can't handle, anyway."

"Maybe he's in love," Emily said impishly. "He's been seeing the school teacher, Hannah Ragsdale, a lot during the past few weeks."

"Is thet it, son?" Ma asked. "She seems like a fine person. Mebbe we should ask her ta dinner."

"No, I'm not in love!" Fred said gruffly. "Hannah's very nice, but we're only friends. I think she enjoys the companionship. There aren't many men her age left. . .since the war."

"I'd guess she's about twenty-five or so," Emily stated. "But that's not old."

"No, it's not," Fred agreed. "She told me she was twenty-five. Her soldier friend was killed at Bull Run, early in the war. They had planned to be married."

"Thet's a shame," Ma said. "We lost so many of our fine young men in thet terrible war. It's only God's grace thet brought ya home ta us, Fred."

"God's been good ta us," Pa added, as he rose from the

table. "Well, Fred. . .ya ready ta get back ta work? We've got ta get thet fence patched down by the creek."

Frederic swallowed his milk and pushed back his chair. "Ready as I'll ever be, Pa. I'll try and keep my mind on the work at hand. Just crack me on the back if I get day-dreamin'."

Emily picked up dirty dishes and carried them to the sink. "Sarah Jane's coming over this afternoon, Ma. She wants me to teach her to sew."

"Land sakes, thet's right. Her ma never did like ta sew. Can't understand it, neither. It's right pleasin' ta take a piece of material and fashion it into a dress. Don't know what I'd do iffen I didn't sew."

After cleaning up the dishes, Emily pulled out some scraps of material to get Sarah started. She had several leftover pieces that were suitable and would make good-sized aprons. Carefully, she arranged them on the bed so Sarah could choose whatever color and pattern caught her eye.

Sarah chose a pale cotton calico with little pink rosebuds splashed on it. "This is beautiful," she cried as she hugged it to her. "Is there enough in this piece for an apron?"

"We'll make it enough," Emily laughed. "We can always use a piece of plain fabric for the ties if we need to."

The two worked steadily, and Emily was impressed with how quickly Sarah learned the fundamentals. "You'll be sewing dresses in no time, Sarah. You seem to have a natural talent for it."

"Thanks, Emily. Ma sews, but she doesn't like to. . .doesn't have the patience for it. She said it would be a terrible chore to teach me, and if you were willing, I should grab at it. She's seen the lovely dresses you've made."

"Ma taught me everything I know," Emily confessed. "And I love sewing. . .so does Cassie. It's hard to understand someone not liking it. We've been brought up by a ma and grandma who loved to sew, and taught us at an early age."

The project was completed sooner than Sarah expected and she eyed it with delight. "It'll be a gift for Ma's birthday next month. Won't she be surprised?"

"She'll be very pleased, especially since you made it yourself."

"You did a lot, Emily. I couldn't have done it alone."

"I only gave instructions. . .you did the real work. I'm really proud of how quickly you learned. We can start a dress for you next week, if you'd like."

"Oh, would you, Emily?"

"Look over my patterns and pick out one you like. Buy the needed material and thread at the fabric shop in town. With my supervision, you are ready to tackle a dress."

Sarah left in high spirits, her apron neatly folded and wrapped securely. On an impulse, she headed Star toward the back pasture, hoping for a glimpse of Frederic. She waved at Mr. Mason, who was heading for the house from the direction of the creek.

"Maybe Fred's over there," she said aloud and pulled the reins to turn Star. "I'll just tell him about my sewing lesson."

She could see Frederic in the distance, bent over mending the fence that had been broken by a storm. Star snorted and Fred looked up, just as Sarah Jane slid to the ground beside him. She kneeled close to see what he was working on. Straying wisps of her red-gold hair fell across his face, and he felt the familiar giddy sensation rising in his veins.

"Can I help, Fred?" she asked. "I've helped Pa mend fences before."

Frederic stood up and pushed back his dark hair, curly and damp from the summer heat. He pulled out a clean bandanna and wiped his face and brow. "Sarah, you do take a body by surprise. How did you know I was here?"

"Just a guess, Fred. Emily taught me to sew today. I made an apron for my ma's birthday, and Emily's planning to help me make a dress next week. Let me help you. Ma doesn't expect me home till supper time."

Frederic handed her a fence rail. "You hold and I'll pound."

She smiled up at him and grabbed the rail firmly. For a moment her limpid blue eyes gazed steadily into his. He felt like a sailor lost in the depths of the sea. As he bent over his work, her hair brushed his face again, and he felt a sudden surge of excitement. Awkwardly, he reached for his tools, fumbled, and dropped them. "What a clumsy oaf! I'll never get this right. Pa will be back and I won't be finished."

"Here, Fred. . .you hold the rail and I'll pound." Sarah reached for the tools and felt his strong hands upon her shoulders. He turned her toward him and gently cupped her face in his hands.

"That's not a good idea, Sarah," he said huskily. He felt her trembling body close to his, and once again suppressed a deep desire to take her in his arms. "You. . .you'd better go home now."

"Am I interfering with your work?" Sarah asked in a disappointed tone. "I only wanted to help."

"I know you did and I appreciate it. But I can't do my work when I get distracted. Run along now."

Sarah climbed on Star and headed home. *"Run along," he said. Like I was a child pestering him. That's all I am to him—a child. That's all I'll ever be, no matter how old I get.* She did not look back at him once. *I've learned my lesson. I won't pester him again.*

Frederic watched her ride away, then turned back to his task with a heavy heart. "What's a fella to do?" he sighed. "I can't fight these feelings much longer. Sarah Jane is so lovely. Whenever she's near me, all I can think about is pulling her into my arms. If only she weren't so young. . ."

thirty

The lengthening days of summer brought busy activity to the Mason household: planting, weeding, nurturing the crops. Harnesses needed to be oiled and mended and the outbuildings cleaned and repaired. Frederic was happiest working in the fields or out in the pasture mending fences.

He had talked Mr. Turner into hiring Peter McClough on a trial basis at the mill, and all reports were good thus far. Peter proved a conscientious young man, willing to do an honest day's work. The Mason family invited him over for dinner often and could see evidence of changes in his life. As they showered him with friendship and concern, his attitude softened and he became less aloof. His gruff and raucous ways were gradually giving way to a more peaceful and gentler nature.

Although they exercised no pressure, the family felt it would not be long before Peter would willingly attend church with them. He had made his peace with man. . .now he needed to be at peace with God.

Peter felt overwhelmed because they referred to him as "family," giving him a feeling of belonging that met a need deep in his heart. He'd had no father's companionship, and his mother had cared little about him. . .had treated him as though he were in the way. The Mason family, on the other hand, made him feel welcome, even wanted, and he found himself anticipating each visit with greater pleasure than the one before. Although not accustomed to farm work, he took pleasure in helping Frederic with chores on each of his visits.

&

Emily wanted Robert Harris to know the facts about her impoverished state, as she called it. At a loss as to how to tell him, she grew more impatient with each passing day. *Is Louisa right? Does Robert love me? If so, there is nothing to keep us apart.* The thought of marriage to Robert gave her a warm, peaceful feeling. *Oh, I've changed a great deal from the saucy young lady that wanted to be "somebody." God, You took me through some difficult times. . .but You showed me it doesn't take wealth and position to be "somebody." It's more important to be "somebody" for You.* "Robert's strong faith will have a strengthening effect on my own," she said aloud. "Together, we will serve God. Yes, together." She emphasized the word and it was a soothing balm to her anxious heart.

A few days later, Robert Harris appeared unexpectedly in the afternoon at the Mason farm. He explained he was making routine visits to members of his congregation, and hoped he was not imposing.

The menfolk were out in the field, but Mrs. Mason was delighted with his presence and bustled about getting them some refreshments. Emily had been baking cookies and quickly pulled back wisps of hair and patted them into place. She took off her apron and felt her heart pounding as she entered the parlor where Robert sat looking at the old family Bible.

"Hello, Robert," she said somewhat breathlessly. "It's so nice of you to call."

Mrs. Mason reappeared with cool drinks and some of Emily's freshly baked cookies. The conversation was light and cheerful, with Robert and Mrs. Mason doing most of the talking. Emily sat quietly with her hands folded in her lap, saying very little, but watching Robert carefully.

Finally, he stood up as if to leave. "Emily. . .would you walk with me for a spell? I'd like to see some of the farm."

Emily was sure her heart skipped a beat. She jumped up, then reprimanded herself for appearing too anxious. "Certainly, Robert," she said calmly. "Let's walk down the back lane to the creek. It's one of my favorite spots."

They walked in silence for a short distance, and Emily thought her heart would burst. *This is a good opportunity to tell him about losing the inheritance. Would I seem brazen and forward?* As she tried to find the right words, she could feel her heart pounding in her bosom.

Robert stopped abruptly in the path, reached for her hand, and faced Emily squarely. "Emily, I. . ." His husky voice took on a serious quality. Suddenly a broad smile spread across his face, turning into the familiar lop-sided grin.

"What is it, Robert?" she demanded.

"My dearest Emily," he chuckled softly, "you are very beautiful—but you have smudges of flour on your nose." Robert pulled out his handkerchief and gently wiped the flour smudges from her face while looking directly into her eyes.

Emily wanted to run away from his teasing smile but felt glued to the spot. His words, "My dearest Emily," kept resounding in her heart.

Robert tucked his handkerchief back into his pocket. "My dearest Emily," he repeated, "I—" His voice faltered, but he continued to look into Emily's eyes steadily. He shook his head, and his grin flickered across his face for a moment. "Here I rehearsed what I came to say so many times—and now I've forgotten every word. You wouldn't think this would be harder than that first sermon I preached here in Waterville, would you? But it is, Emily."

He took a deep breath and tried again. "What I want to say—what I came here to say is—I care for you deeply, Emily.

I know we haven't had a courtship as such, probably I'm putting the cart before the horse by saying all this before I've courted you properly. But ever since that first time I saw you, that time you fell on the ice, I've been sure of my feelings for you. I couldn't court you then, though. How could I when you would barely speak to me back then? Do you remember?"

Once again, Emily saw his lop-sided grin, but his eyes still looked seriously into hers. "I couldn't very well court you when you wouldn't even let me call you by your first name, now could I?"

Emily blushed, but her eyes were glowing with happiness. Robert's eyes searched her face. "When your aunt died, you had so much to deal with, you were hurting so badly, that I didn't want to press myself on you then. I knew you needed time to heal, to straighten out things with God. But I wanted so badly to put my arms around you and comfort you. And then I found out your aunt had left you her house and money. I couldn't court you then. I was afraid you would think I was interested in you for the wrong reasons. And my pride got in the way. I could bring you nothing at all, while you already had so much. I pulled away then, tried to hide my feelings away inside myself."

He looked down at her, traced the oval of her face with one finger. "When Louisa told me you no longer have an inheritance, I was glad. That's an awful thing to say, isn't it? But it's true. For the first time, I felt as though nothing was standing between us." He drew in his breath. "I decided I'd better tell you how I felt right away, before something else came up to separate us. I love you, Emily. And you're just looking up at me, smiling, but you haven't said a word. Does that smile possibly mean you could care for me?"

Emily's smile grew wider. "Oh, yes, Robert. I care for you a great deal."

He drew her close and his lips brushed hers gently. Then he pulled back and grinned. "It's your turn now to talk. Tell me why you pushed me away when you first met me. Tell me what you thought. Tell me everything."

Emily looked away from his gaze, and her cheeks grew rosy. "I think I was attracted to you right from the first, too. But I was afraid I had looked like a fool that day when I fell on the ice. I was afraid you were laughing at me."

"I would never do that."

"Unless of course I had flour on my face."

Robert grinned. "Of course. But keep talking. I want to know everything."

"Well," Emily looked through the trees to where the sunlight flickered on the creek, "I didn't like thinking someone might laugh at me. I was taking myself very seriously in those days, you see, and so I was angry with you. And I tried to regain my dignity by being very cool toward you. But I couldn't resist you for very long. During the Christmas program, you were so good with the children. And you were always dropping by Aunt Maude's and talking about my courses with me. I found myself thinking about you more and more. But when Aunt Maude died, I was so angry with God. I was hurting so bad I didn't want to let anyone close, not you, not even my own family."

She looked up at him, and her lips curved. "But it was your wisdom and gentleness that helped me heal, that helped me be able to come to God again. Only then I was sure you could never. . .care for someone who had been so full of doubts. After all, you're a preacher and. . ." Her voice trailed away.

"You think preachers never have any doubts?"

"Do they?"

He nodded. "Everyone does sometimes. But no matter how many times we waver, God never does. And that's all that matters." Once again, he pulled her close.

After a few moments, they drew apart and walked together down the path arm in arm, feeling a contented closeness.

"I'm sorry you lost the money for your schooling," he said after a moment. "I know I told you I was glad you lost your inheritance—but I'm truly sorry about your having to leave school. I know how important it was to you."

"Don't be sorry for me, Robert," she said hugging his arm. "I couldn't be happier than I am at this moment. I wouldn't want the inheritance. . .not if it meant losing you."

He stood still in the path and looked down at her. "After all these months of loving you from afar, I can hardly believe this is happening. I can hardly believe I'm hearing you say what you are." She saw him swallow and then take another deep breath. "I'm tempted to ask you what I really want to ask you right now. But I want us to have a courtship, Emily," he said. "It's important because I want you to be sure. My feelings for you will never change. But I realize the life of a pastor's wife can be a difficult one. It's something that needs a great deal of thought. I may be called to a pastorate far away from Waterville. I hope not. . .I love it here. But if God calls me, I must go."

Emily had never considered the possibility that marriage to Robert might take her away from her beloved family. She set her shoulders squarely, though, knowing her place would always be at this man's side. "Do. . .do you think I would make a good pastor's wife?"

Robert looked down at her sweet, upturned face. . .radiant and full of love. Leaning over, he gently kissed her hair and held her close. "Yes, I do, my darling," he said huskily. "You'd be the very best."

thirty-one

In July, Frederic, with his father's help, started clearing timber on a small wooded knoll overlooking the creek. This was the spot he'd selected before the war for his future cabin. It lay not too far back from the main house and outbuildings, yet was somewhat secluded. They cleared only those trees needed for a sizeable cabin, leaving the others untouched.

"It's the perfect spot for me, Pa, here in the woods. I like the quietness of it back here. Just the lowing of the cattle from the pasture, the songs of the birds, and the croaking of the bullfrogs. This will be my haven of peace."

"Yep, son, it shore be a pretty spot. Yer ma will miss havin' ya at the big house, though. She loves ta fuss over ya. While ya were away at the war, she fretted a lot about yer safety. She'd say, 'When our boy comes home, then things will be right in the world agin.' She shore enjoys cookin' all yer favorites."

Frederic laughed. "She sure does, Pa, and I love eating them. No one cooks like Ma does."

"Well, son, even if ya want this cabin of yer own, ya can still take yer meals with us. Yer ma wouldn't have it any other way. It's gonna be hard on her. Emily and Robert Harris are courtin' now. There might be a weddin' next summer. Cassie's weddin' was hard enough, even though we still had Emily, and ya'd come back ta us from the war."

Frederic stacked the last log, wiped the sweat from his brow, and hobbled over to his pa, settling down on a grassy spot beside him. "Ma will do fine, Pa. You'll see. Remember,

153

there's a new baby coming around Christmas. Can't you just picture Ma with her grandchild? Can't you just see her fussin' and spoilin' the little one?"

"Thet'll be somethin'," Pa agreed. "Fact is, we'll all be a spoilin' him. . .or her, whichever the good Lord sends."

The dinner bell tolled in the distance, telling them the evening meal was ready.

"I knew it was time ta quit when I set down here," Pa said from his spot on the ground. "My belly reminded me thet it was supper time. Let's go git it, son."

They gathered their tools and headed down the trail toward the house, with Laddie at their heels.

"We accomplished a lot, Pa. Thanks for your help."

"Yep, we did. But it's slow goin', son. We did a full day's work taday and thet's a good feelin'. There's no hurry, is there?" He gave his son a keen glance.

Fred shook his head. "Just so's it's done by November, before winter sets in. I want to have it buttoned up by then."

"Any partickler reason ya've decided ya need yer own place, son? Wouldn't have anything to do with that pretty teacher friend of yers?"

Again Frederic shook his head. "No, Pa, like I've said before, Hannah and I are just friends."

Chase's eyes rested on his son's face. "Well, ya got something—or someone—on your mind, I can tell. I have a feelin' ya are buildin' this cabin for someone special. But I won't press ya. Ya tell me when ya're ready, son. And in the meantime, we'll be gettin' this cabin ready."

Frederic followed his father down the trail. He looked back once at the cabin, still visible through the tree trunks. He was building it for someone all right, or at least he hoped he was. But so far, he could only admit that to himself, and that was hard enough. He frowned, forcing himself to face the thought that after all he might be the only one who would live in the new cabin. Emily had said Sarah was in love with him—but now Emily said Sarah was seeing a boy her own age. *What if I've fallen in love with Sarah*, Frederic thought, *just when she's fallen out of love with me?* He shook his head, still uncomfortable with the thought that he might be in love with Sarah Jane, a girl so much younger than himself.

But before he and his father reached the house, Frederic looked back one more time in the direction of the cabin. He knew without a doubt his father was right: he was building the little house for someone, and that someone was on his mind every minute that he worked on the cabin. The cabin would be his haven of peace one day—but only if he could share it with someone special. And in spite of himself, his heart insisted that Sarah Jane Collins was that special someone.

❧

Mrs. Mason had supper waiting for them. Peter McClough had stopped by and been persuaded to join them. After washing up, Fred and his father met with the others at the table.

"Glad ya dropped by ta join us, Peter," Pa said, passing him a large platter of ham. "We hope ya allus feel welcome here."

"I do feel welcome, Mr. Mason, and I appreciate your generosity. You folks have been kind to a lonely orphan. . .much kinder than I deserved."

"How's the job at the mill, Peter?" Fred asked. "Is the work pretty hard?"

"It's hard enough. . .but it's good for me."

Fred buttered a chunk of homemade bread. "You don't have to work, do you? Couldn't you just live off your inheritance?"

"I could, Fred. I don't need the money. . .I have more than enough. It's a strange feeling knowing I don't have to work. I guess I like the job better because I know I don't have to do it. The work keeps me occupied so I'm not lonely in that big house. Makes the time pass quickly."

"Peter, ya jest come visit us whenever ya feel lonely," Ma said. "We like havin' another youngun around."

"I'm planning to build my own cabin back by the creek," Fred mentioned. "The logs will come off our own property, but I'll be coming in to town to the mill for some building supplies soon. I hope to have most of it completed before winter."

"Can I help?" Peter asked enthusiastically. "I could give you a hand and learn a lot in the process."

"I'll welcome all the help I can get, Peter. But aren't you busy most of the day? We don't work on Sundays."

"I could help after work and I always have one weekday off. I'll squeeze in all the time I can. Sounds like a challenge."

"Ya can take yer meals with us when ya come," Ma said. "I can allus set an extra plate."

"Thanks, Mrs. Mason. Fred, why do you want a place of your own? You have the best right here." Peter glanced around the table at the family.

"Well, you have your own place, Peter. It will be a good feeling, at my age, to be on my own. . .but close enough for Ma's home cookin'." Fred winked and smiled fondly at his mother.

"At your age, Fred," Emily mimicked. "You sound like you are an old man!"

"I'm sure Peter would agree with me when I say the war aged us. I'm ready to move, just so it's on this property . . .back by the creek. I picked the spot out before I joined up with the Union troops. It's so quiet and peaceful back there."

"It always was your favorite spot," Emily agreed. "But

won't you be lonely? Peter admits he is."

"Naw. I'll have all the wildlife around. Anyway, I'll be here at the big house most of the time, I reckon."

"Emily," Peter said, "I've hired Martha to come in once a week and clean for me. She's a very capable and thorough person. The day she comes, she fixes my supper and leaves it on the stove. That's the best food I ever get, except when I come here." Peter took a second helping of ham and potatoes. "Mrs. Mason, you are by far the best cook around!"

He chewed his food thoughtfully for a few moments. "Folks, I came out here tonight for a special reason. You've all been more than kind to me and now I want to do something for all of you. Emily, there is money set aside for you to go on to school. Your Aunt Maude wanted it that way, and I'm sure Uncle George, my pa, would have agreed. Fred, I can help you with physical labor whenever possible on your log home, but I also want to buy your needed building materials. For Bill and Cassie, I'd already planned to give them a substantial money gift for the coming baby. And for you, Mr. and Mrs. Mason and Grandpa. . ."

"Now jest wait a minute, young feller," Grandpa said. "We old folks don't need a thing."

The rest of the family sat spellbound. Emily recovered first. "That is a very kind offer, Peter, but I'm not sure if I want to go back to school."

"The money is there for you," Peter said seriously. "Isn't schooling what you always wanted?"

"Yes, it is. But there have been some changes in my life. I would have to pray about it and give it a great deal of thought."

"I couldn't take any money for building supplies," Fred murmured. "It's rightfully your money, Peter, and we don't expect a cent."

"I know you don't. But can't you accept it as a gift. . .a

repayment for all the kindnesses shown me? I have more than I need and would like to share. It isn't a loan I'm talking about. It's a free gift."

Grandpa cleared his throat. "Thet free gift ya mentioned reminds us of God's love and His free gift ta us. . .the gift of eternal life through Jesus Christ, His Son. Have ya ever accepted God's gift, Peter?"

Peter looked down at his plate. He felt strange and uncomfortable. Something was going on inside him that he didn't understand. Usually any talk about God or religion angered him.

God never bothered about me. I grew up without a father. My loose-living mother never showed me any love. But I see love in this family. . .the way they care for one another . . .the way they care about me. I've been such a rotten character all my life. Could there really be a God somewhere Who loves me?

thirty-two

Peter's thoughts were troubled. He'd felt an uneasiness ever since his visit to the Masons and Grandpa's talk about God's free gift. The family had not pressed him or forced their beliefs on him, and for that he was grateful. He had none of the bitter feelings he'd often felt in the past when someone mentioned God; instead, he had a gnawing ache deep inside, as though something was missing in his life. Whenever it was convenient, he joined Frederic, his pa, and his grandpa to work on the cabin. Cassie's Bill and his pa, Mr. Collins, also lent a hand whenever possible.

By the end of September, the cabin was completed on the outside and able to stand against the elements of nature. The setting by the creek was impressive. Autumn had arrived with the Master Painter's brilliant splashes of color. Towering trees bedecked in red, orange, and gold stood gracefully among the green pines.

"Kinda takes your breath away," Peter said one Saturday, standing back to survey the picturesque setting. "I can see why you picked this particular spot, Fred. It's outstanding."

"I know. Words really can't describe it. Only God could create such beauty. . .and give it to us to enjoy. We don't deserve all the good things He pours out upon us every day."

Peter muttered something under his breath and turned away. He couldn't understand this family. They gave God the credit for every good thing that happened to them. And if there were difficulties. . .things they couldn't work out, they insisted God still cared about them and was in control.

I feel pulled in two directions. Maybe this God is on the level and does love everyone, good or bad, the same. Could this be what I'm missing in my life? Money hasn't been the answer. Oh, it's nice to have, but it doesn't satisfy my longing deep inside. Naw, it can't be as simple as that. Just accept God's free gift, through His Son, they say. If I could see God, really see Him in person, then I'd know He is real. Maybe. . .maybe then I'd be ready to accept His free gift.

"Peter," Fred's voice broke into his thoughts. "Let's join the others for lunch. Ma's probably waiting on us."

The two young men walked side by side down the trail toward the house.

"Zack Turner thinks highly of you, Fred," Peter stated. "It's a fact."

"Well, I think highly of him also. We've been good friends for a long time."

"I heard about what happened. . .how he stole your girl while you were at the war."

"That was two-sided, Peter. Becky Sue heard the news about my wounded leg." Fred moved his hand up and down, massaging his bad leg. "She was sure I was going to lose it. I guess she couldn't handle that."

"Didn't you hate Zack and Becky Sue for what they did? He'd be my enemy. I'd have gone after him and beat him to a pulp."

"Would that have solved anything, Peter?"

"No. . .but it would have given me a heap of satisfaction."

"I don't think it would in the long run. The Bible tells us to love our enemies and forgive them. What's to be gained by a fight? I'd have lost Zack's friendship. Anyway, they were already married and that can't be changed."

"Would you change it now if you could?"

"I'm not in love with Becky Sue any more. Maybe it was

just an infatuation. Sometimes God changes our plans. But I know He works things out for the best."

"Your mind is on the school teacher now, isn't it? I understand you've been courting her."

"I wouldn't call it courting, Peter. We've gone for walks in the park, attended some band concerts and a few picnics. Hannah is a fine person. She's easy to talk to and I'm comfortable around her."

"Sounds rather dull," Peter said. "Aren't there any sparks there?"

Frederic laughed. "Not the kind you mean. We're good friends who enjoy each other's company. Hannah suggested we keep our relationship on a strictly friendly basis, and that suited me fine. What about you, Peter? Is there a fair maiden who has caught your eye?"

Peter shrugged. "I'm not sure any lady would look kindly on attention from me. I'm just a nobody."

Frederic put an arm lightly around Peter's shoulder. "You're somebody very special to God, Peter. He likes you just the way you are."

"Maybe so," Peter mumbled. "Maybe so."

"Peter, I didn't want you to buy all those building supplies. You sure work your way around a fella, bringing them out on your own. Thanks. You're a good friend."

Peter's face brightened. "I knew you wouldn't accept any money. It's one way I can help."

The two friends entered the kitchen where the others were gathered for the noon meal. After a hearty lunch, the men were eager to resume work on finishing the inside of the cabin.

"Ya men will need ta quit work early," Ma said, "ta be ready fer the potluck supper at church tonight. Why don't ya come with us, Peter?"

"Naw, I've never been inside a church. I wouldn't know

how to act."

"Just be yerself," Ma insisted. "It's a git-acquainted time for meetin' new people. Ya'd be more'n welcome and they'd all make ya feel right at home."

The others urged Peter to join them and he finally agreed. "Hope God won't be too surprised to see me in church," he quipped.

"I'll introduce you to Hannah," Frederic said. "You'll enjoy talking to her."

The men finished work on the cabin early so they could clean up for the church potluck. Peter met them at the church, somewhat ill at ease. "Do I look proper?" he asked Fred as they entered the building.

"You look fine."

"What do I say to people?"

"Don't worry about what to say. The folks here are all friendly. They'll do most of the talking. As Ma said, just be yourself."

Frederic introduced Peter to several people, then seated him across from Hannah at one of the tables. "This is my cousin, Peter McClough."

Hannah took up the conversation, as Frederic knew she would, and kept Peter's attention during the meal. After dinner, chairs were moved into a semicircle and the group joined in a time of singing. Hannah seated herself between Peter and Frederic. "Peter," she said, turning to him, "you aren't singing."

"Naw, I can't sing," Peter said awkwardly. "I hoped no one would notice."

"Of course you can," Hannah said handing him a song book. She smiled and turned to the correct page. Peter felt drawn to this cultured and self-assured young woman. She was pretty and her inner beauty drew him like a magnet. He looked over at Frederic, but Fred seemed intent on watching someone across the semicircle.

Peter turned to follow Fred's gaze and saw the young Collins girl. He had noticed glances passing between Fred and her during the meal. When she smiled at Fred, Peter watched emotion rise in his friend's face. *Frederic is completely unaware that Hannah and I are even here. He has eyes only for Sarah Collins. Could he be in love with her? Does he know how much his face reveals?*

These thoughts haunted Peter and kept him awake into the long hours of the night. "It seems Fred and Hannah really are just friends," he mumbled. "I wonder. . .I wonder if she would consider allowing me to call. When she looked at me. . .I thought she looked like she might like me."

He rolled over and pressed his face against the pillow. *And if someone like Hannah could like me, then maybe it's true what Frederic said about God. Maybe He really does like me just the way I am. . .*

&

The next day when he finished work, Peter strolled past the house where Hannah boarded. He was trying hard to appear casual, but his shoulders were stiff with tension. As he drew closer to the house, he saw that Hannah was seated on the porch, and he was filled with both relief and nervousness.

"Why, hello, there," he called, hoping his voice sounded calm and friendly.

Hannah stood up and came to lean on the porch railing. "Hello, Peter. How nice to see you again so soon. Would you like to come sit down and have a glass of lemonade?"

"Sure sounds good," Peter said, smiling.

He climbed the porch steps and seated himself in one of the wooden rocking chairs that sat on the porch. Hannah went to get the lemonade and soon returned with a tall, cool glass.

Peter took a long swallow. "Mmm. Thank you. This surely hits the spot after a long day's work."

"How do you like your work at the mill?"

"I'm enjoying it. It helps fill my time. I enjoy working with the men."

"Do you get lonely living in that big house by yourself?"

Peter leaned back in the chair. "Yes, I do." He looked at Hannah's face and saw the genuine interest in her eyes. "I never thought I would. When I came here, I was so filled up with angry feelings, I didn't think I'd need anything except money and a nice place to live. I thought finally not having to worry about money would be all I'd need to make me happy. I found out I was wrong." He clenched and unclenched his hands, ashamed to admit these things to the gentle, cultured Hannah; somehow, though, being honest with her seemed important.

"I've learned a lot from the Masons," he said after a moment. "I never met anyone like them before. I never had no family of my own, not that cared anything about me. My ma didn't amount to much and I never knew my pa." He shot a glance at Hannah's face again, waiting to see a look of shocked withdrawal, but he read only sympathetic concern in her eyes. "I expected the Masons to hate me—after all, I'd taken their aunt's money from them. And I'd known Frederic during the war—he and I didn't get along, and it was my own fault, I have to confess. Something about him always seemed to rile me—I guess the way he always seemed so at peace with himself and with God. So I came here ready to fight the Masons."

Peter drained the last of his lemonade and set the glass down on the small table that stood between his chair and Hannah's. He shook his head. "Instead, they've welcomed me like I was really one of the family. They actually seem to like me."

Hannah smiled. "I can see why they do."

Peter felt his face flush. "I've never been somebody that people liked."

Hannah looked away from his face for a moment. "I think," she said after a moment, "that we all need people to accept us just the way we are. And then we *become* likeable even if we weren't before. Maybe you were so angry inside—and so unpleasant outside—because you'd never met people who just liked you as you were."

Peter leaned toward her. "Funny, Frederic was saying something like that to me the other day. Only he was talking about . . ." Peter cleared his throat nervously. "He was talking about God."

Hannah smiled. "God loves us just the way we are. Sometimes I find that hard to believe—"

"You do?" Peter asked, surprised that this lovely and composed woman would ever have feelings of doubt.

Hannah nodded. "But He really does love us." She reached across the space between them and quickly, gently touched his hand. "He really does love you."

Peter felt the warmth of her brief touch linger on his hand. *Maybe, just maybe, you don't have to see God to know He loves you,* he thought. *Maybe you can see His love through other people. People like the Masons. And like Hannah.*

Peter cleared his throat. "Uh, Hannah?"

"Yes?"

"Could I call on you again. . .sometime soon?"

"I'd like that, Peter. I'd like that very much."

thirty-three

In early October, the Masons invited the Collins family, Robert Harris, and Peter McClough for a harvest dinner. Becky Sue and Zack were invited too, but they were unable to attend because their young baby had a cold. Cassie had especially looked forward to holding the little one. "What a disappointment," she said. "I wanted to cuddle little Zack. He's such a sweet baby."

"You'll soon be cuddling your own, Cassie," Emily exclaimed. "Only a couple months to go."

"We can hardly wait," Bill commented. "It will change our lives having a little one in the house."

"I plan to spoil him," Emily said saucily.

"Or spoil her, don't you mean?" Robert asked.

"Whichever. . .," Emily sighed in anticipation. "He or she will be spoiled by their Aunt Emily, that's for certain."

While the others discussed the coming baby, Frederic watched Sarah's face. Was she avoiding him, he wondered; she seemed to be looking everywhere except at him. He hadn't talked to her in a long time now, not since that day when she had offered to help him with the fence post and he had longed so badly to take her in his arms. Had he frightened her away? Or was she busy with a beau, someone her own age?

For weeks now, Frederic had been unable to put Sarah out of his mind. She filled his thoughts day and night, and finally he had been forced to admit to himself that despite the difference in their ages, he had fallen in love with her. Lately, instead of lying awake tormenting himself with fears and hopeless longing, he had been praying about his feelings for Sarah. Now, he had finally reached a feeling of peace. And he was pretty certain he knew what God wanted him to do.

He smiled to himself, just as Sarah's eyes turned toward him. Their gazes caught and held, and he watched her cheeks flush. He leaned across the table toward her and said softly, "Let's go for a walk after dinner, Sarah. It's a nice day for one."

"Yes, it is, Frederic," she said breathlessly, the color rising still higher in her cheeks. "A walk would be fine." Excitement built within her until she picked at her food, barely able to swallow.

After dinner Frederic nodded to her, put his finger to his lips, and jerked his head toward the door.

"I'll go get my wrap," she said quietly, "and meet you outside."

Frederic was limping toward the back land when she caught up with him a few minutes later. The fall day was sunny with a cool nip in the air. The trees were brilliantly arrayed in their full panorama of color. Some of the leaves fluttered down, forming a carpet on the ground that crunched under their feet as they walked.

"What a glorious day, Frederic. I guess fall is my favorite time of the year."

"Mine too," Frederic said thoughtfully, taking a long sideways glance at his companion. Her cheeks were flushed and her curly red-gold tresses bounced about her shoulders as she walked. Frederic could feel his heart thumping wildly within his chest.

"Pa's been telling me about your cabin," Sarah said. "Pa says it's big and mighty nice."

"I think so," Frederic agreed. "Would you like to see it? It's just over this hill and down by the creek."

Sarah clapped her hands in delight. "Oh, yes, I would . . .very much."

They came to the clearing in a grove of pines where the cabin nestled. Sarah took a deep breath. "What a beautiful cabin, Frederic. There's something special about a log home. And I love the smell of new wood."

"The porch overlooks the back pasture and also the creek," Frederic said, excitement rising in his voice. "And the sunsets. . .well, they are magnificent."

Sarah stood on the porch, dreamily gazing at the landscape.

"Come inside, Sarah," Frederic called, "and see the layout of the rooms. Everything is finished except for the furnishings."

Sarah walked through the house quietly, taking it all in. Suddenly her voice became sad. "I guess this is the house you planned for Becky Sue. . ." A little sob caught in her throat and she looked away. "It's just too bad. . .," her voice trailed off.

"Long ago I did plan on building this house for Becky Sue," Frederic said seriously. "But instead, I built this house with someone else in mind."

Sarah Jane turned to him with tears filling her eyes. "So you do plan to get married, then? We've all been wondering about that. . .why you'd build a place of your own!" Her voice broke and she struggled to go on. "The talk about you and Miss Ragsdale must be true. Everyone says you two are going to be married. I know you've been courting her these past months." She turned abruptly, ran out of the house and blindly down the path.

"Wait, Sarah Jane!" Frederic called as he limped after her. "Wait!"

Sarah kept running, choking back her tears, leaving Frederic far behind.

"It's for you, Sarah Jane," he called loudly and his words echoed across the valley. "I built the cabin for you!"

Instantly, she halted, then turned and ran back to him. She put her hands on her hips and stared at him, her red-gold curls blowing in the wind. "What are you talking about, Frederic Mason?" Her voice trembled.

He took a step closer to her. "I'm talking about wanting to marry you, Sarah Jane Collins." His voice was soft and husky. "I know maybe I waited too long to realize how I felt about you. And then I had to get up my courage to talk to you. By now you've probably found someone your own age, someone who's made you realize—"

Sarah reached out a small fist and thumped his chest. "Will you be quiet? You're the only one I want, the only one I've ever wanted. . ." Her voice faltered and she blinked tears out of her eyes, then grinned mischievously and added, "Even if you are old enough to be my grandfather. Or you'd think so from the way you talk."

He reached out, took her in his arms, and held her close against his chest. "I've wanted to do this for a long time," he whispered against her hair.

She pulled away and looked up at him. Her face, streaked with tears, wore a brilliant smile. "You really built the cabin for me?" she asked breathlessly. Her violet-blue eyes searched his.

"For you, my darling," he said huskily, drawing her close once more. He gently kissed her tear-stained face. "I love you, Sarah Jane. I want you to marry me. Will you?"

He saw her answer in her eyes, and then his lips met hers. After a long moment, they turned back toward the cabin, and hand in hand, they walked through it once more.

Frederic took a deep breath, hardly daring to believe Sarah's hand was really in his. He remembered the long, hard days during the war, and then the pain, both physical and emotional, that had followed. The war was over, though; God had brought him safely through all the danger and pain.

And now at last, God had given him this home of his own to share with Sarah. Together they would build their own haven of peace.

A Letter To Our Readers

Dear Reader:

In order that we might better contribute to your reading enjoyment, we would appreciate your taking a few minutes to respond to the following questions. When completed, please return to the following:

Rebecca Germany, Editor
Heartsong Presents
P.O. Box 719
Uhrichsville, Ohio 44683

1. Did you enjoy reading *Haven of Peace*?
   ❑ Very much. I would like to see more books
      by this author!
   ❑ Moderately
      I would have enjoyed it more if _____

   _____

2. Are you a member of *Heartsong Presents*? Yes   No
   If no, where did you purchase this book? _____

   _____

3. What influenced your decision to purchase this
   book? (Check those that apply.)

   ❑ Cover   ❑ Back cover copy

   ❑ Title   ❑ Friends

   ❑ Publicity   ❑ Other _____

4. On a scale from 1 (poor) to 10 (superior), please rate the following elements.

    ___Heroine   ___Plot

    ___Hero   ___Inspirational theme

    ___Setting   ___Secondary characters

5. What settings would you like to see covered in *Heartsong Presents* books?

_____

_____

6. What are some inspirational themes you would like to see treated in future books?_____

_____

_____

7. Would you be interested in reading other *Heartsong Presents* titles?   ❑ Yes   ❑ No

8. Please check your age range:
❑ Under 18   ❑ 18-24   ❑ 25-34
❑ 35-45   ❑ 46-55   ❑ Over 55

9. How many hours per week do you read? _____

Name _____

Occupation _____

Address _____

City _____ State _____ Zip _____

Introducing New Authors!

Page Winship Dooly
___Heart's Desire___—Cole Wilder agrees to escort Hannah to her aunt's home in Missouri. Will their journey end in a handshake or will they realize in time their hearts' desire? HP84 $2.95

Loree Lough
___Pocketful of Love___—Out of their sorrow a friendship develops, and the possiblility of love. However, vengeful enemies and jealous rivals determine to destroy the bloom of happiness Elice and Cabot have found in each other's arms. HP86 $2.95

Carolyn R. Scheidies
___To Be Strong___—Now that she can walk again, Kit Anderson longs for God's total healing. Instead, He calls her to face still greater challenges. Her doubts seem to flee when Dr. Keith Long helps her understand the reality of God's love. HP94 $2.95

Carol Mason Parker
___Haven of Peace___—When Frederic Mason returns home from the Civil War, he finds that his fiancée has married another man. As he finds God revealed in the beauty of the land, his heart heals, but he is certainly not ready for a relationship with Sarah Jane. HP104 $2.95

···Hearts ♥ng···

······· Presents ·······

Great Inspirational Romance at a Great Price!

Heartsong Presents books are inspirational romances in contemporary and historical settings, designed to give you an enjoyable, spirit-lifting reading experience. You can choose from 104 wonderfully written titles from some of today's best authors like Colleen L. Reece, Brenda Bancroft, Janelle Jamison, and many others.

When ordering quantities less than twelve, above titles are $2.95 each.

Heartsong Presents
Love Stories Are Rated G!

That's for godly, gratifying, and of course, great! If you love a thrilling love story, but don't appreciate the sordidness of popular paperback romances, **Heartsong Presents** is for you. In fact, **Heartsong Presents** is the *only inspirational romance book club*, the only one featuring love stories where Christian faith is the primary ingredient in a marriage relationship.

Sign up today to receive your first set of four, never before published Christian romances. Send no money now; you will receive a bill with the first shipment. You may cancel at any time without obligation, and if you aren't completely satisfied with any selection, you may return the books for an immediate refund!

Imagine. . .four new romances every month—two historical, two contemporary—with men and women like you who long to meet the one God has chosen as the love of their lives. . .all for the low price of $9.97 postpaid.

To join, simply complete the coupon below and mail to the address provided. **Heartsong Presents** romances are rated G for another reason: They'll arrive *Godspeed!*